THE CIGARETTE GIRL ON THE *TANGO*

BY

D. J. PHINNEY

ARROYO WILLOW
PRESS

THE CIGARETTE GIRL ON THE *TANGO*

Arroyo Willow Press

Publisher's Note: This is a work of fiction. Names, characters, places, and incidents are a product of the author's imagination. Locales and public names are sometimes used for atmospheric purposes. Any resemblance to actual people, living or dead, or to businesses, companies, events, institutions, or locales is completely coincidental.

Paperback 978-1-7329034-1-8

mobi 978-1-7329034-3-2

ePub 978-1-7329034-4-9

KDP Paperback 978-1-7329034-5-6

For Sharon, Nate, Kelly, Jonas, Anders, and Sunny.

You make me happy when skies are gray.

CHAPTER I

SANTA ANA: THURSDAY, MARCH 3, 1938

For the first time in eight days, sunlight stabbed between the thunderheads, and Willie's instincts told him that Elena was in trouble.

The rains had calmed. Willie stood atop the porch steps facing Tenth Street. Murky waters smothered tree-lined lanes of uptown Santa Ana. Pouring through Floral Park, the floods had toppled Mr. Hager's Chevrolet Deluxe, had washed out all of Mrs. Pike's new picket fences. Willie paced, hands in his pockets. He had to check up on Elena.

He'd never sleep until he knew she had survived.

No one was sure how bad these floods were. There'd been no signals on the radio for forty-seven hours. KVOE had gone off-air. The local trolleys had stopped running. There were no newspapers. No milk deliveries. No trucks or even cars on roads a full foot underwater. Even the cot in the garage where

Willie lived was drenched from flooding. Still, Mildred ordered him to wring his rain-soaked bedroll out and sleep there.

Sprinkles spattered Willie's arms. Another interlude of rain. He wiped his shoes on her porch welcome mat, pushed open the front door. He made his way into the parlor. Smelled something burning in the kitchen, Mildred sacrificing something. *Hardly mattered, Willie thought. She'd never seat him at her table. She said she knew something about him, and whatever it was set that woman off.*

He had no status. One thing Mildred cared a lot about was status. She wanted movie stars for stepchildren. Claimed Willie looked Neanderthal. Behind his back she called him Tarzan. There was nothing he could do, except move out, which was probably what Mildred had in mind, even though he paid her cash each month to sleep in her garage.

"Where were you going, Willie?" Mildred's voice came squawking from her kitchen.

He didn't answer. He didn't care to answer Mildred anymore. He was nineteen. She didn't love his father. Mildred only used the man, *used* Willie as her errand boy when Pop wasn't around.

Fearing Elena was in danger, Willie stepped outside again. He couldn't stand it any longer. He nudged the front door shut behind him. He rolled his trousers up an inch below his knees. He had to find her. *Nuts to Mildred.* Elena lived up by the Santa Ana River. If Santa Ana's streets were flooded, Elena's home was *underwater*. She'd be terrified. He needed to be with her, hold her, calm her, feel the warmth she always brought him when she shook out her dark hair, smiled wide, and made him feel like a man somebody cared about.

Dark clouds pinched against the sunrays. No time to dawdle any longer. Another storm was coming. Willie waded outward from the porch, leaving Mildred's shrieks behind, a welcome change in his opinion. His pop lived with that harpy he had picked up at the Santa Ana Country Club last autumn when he'd had too much to drink. After Thanksgiving, the old man had moved into Mildred's house, charged Willie rent, and made him sleep in her garage.

Now it was flooded.

Mildred was plain but made it crystal clear the bungalow was *hers*. Pop was a welder at Pacific Electric's trolley barns, downtown. He had no means to buy a house in the Depression. He worked hard to pay the bills for Mildred, plus he payed her mortgage and expenses. That plus Willie's cash kept Mildred in the latest styles from Buffums. Pop and Mildred shared a bedroom. Mildred called it their "arrangement". Willie called it what it was. Pop had no stones, and he was pussy-whipped, except when he got drunk, and took his troubles out on Willie.

Worse, Mildred didn't like Elena. She said it bothered her that Willie dated Mexicans. Or Catholics. Or anything that wasn't Presbyterian. Or British. Mildred Kent would strut around with her nose so high in the air Willie had struggled not to tell her someone ought to mount a cross onto the tip of it with bolts just like those church steeples downtown. That way they'd see her from all over Santa Ana.

He hoped the deluge was receding. A lake of mud covered the neigborhood. It squooshed through Willie's Goodrich P.F. Flyers as he walked. The musty air outside her house smelled like a septic tank gone rancid. He wished he hadn't worn Elena's watch. He feared the floods might ruin it, but knowing how she cared for him, he felt obliged to wear it.

Hurrying north, Willie staggered up the flooded walks of Flower Street in shock. Cars at the curbs had water covering their hubcaps. If Santa Ana looked this bad, what might have happened to his girlfriend and her grandfather in Atwood? Willie's heart rose in his throat.

A roar thundered from the bridge a block away.

Willie didn't like the sound of this.

At all.

Ahead, the surging Santiago Creek descended through the balusters of concrete and had scoured half the asphalt out from Flower Street. Silt swirled off the bridge deck and cascaded through a gully where the rains worked extra hard to undermine concrete abutments. The storms had settled to a drizzle, but several feet of showers in one week had bloated creeks draining the Santa Ana Mountains. The swollen-crazy torrent sent vibrations through his sneakers. He faced the bridge then glanced upstream, fearing his nerves might hold him back.

The banks of Santiago Creek were littered with green citrus branches, lumber ripped from farm buildings, mangled logs from fallen oaks and manzanitas. Muddy runoff topped the bridge deck. Eucalyptus logs were packed against the bridge rail, forcing flow toward an abutment where a Model T had somehow jammed its way into the opening.

Thank heaven. Willie saw no one inside it.

It appeared the bridge would fail before nightfall.

But right now, he had to cross it. He made a leap across the gorge by the abutment to the car roof and then lunged onto the bridge deck. He fought the current on the deck, staggered north, and clawed the rain-soaked concrete railing. Hugging the balustrade, he muscled through the flooding. A man needed to find the girl he loved. Elena needed him. She loved him.

Willie loved Elena even more.

He was muscular and nearly six feet tall. His huge hands

clung to the wet rails. Twice, he almost lost his footing.

He barely made it.

On the north bank, Willie panted as he shivered to stay warm. He caught his breath, watching the carcass of a calf wash past that car he had just stepped on and continue through the gap and on downriver.

The single ray of sun had disappeared.

Willie bent over. Checked his Elgin watch. Ten minutes until three. He was surprised it was still working. It was damp after that Santiago Creek crossing. He'd received it from Elena on his birthday in December in a red box with green ribbons, *plus* her plate of fresh *tamales*, *plus* her photograph with lipstick she had bought for the occasion. Willie had never felt so special.

"It was Papi's lucky watch," Elena'd told him. "Now is yours. Papi used to wear it all the time."

Willie'd looked up. "Uh, what about the night he died?"

She'd choked up. "One night, for some reason...." He could still see Elena's eyes, wider than walnuts, "...Papi left it in the drawer beside his bed table. There are reasons I am begging you to wear it. Is *especial*."

She'd flashed Willie that smile no man could ever disagree with.

That's when she'd told him the police found Papi's corpse on Seal Beach, and she had cried again, and Willie'd held her tight until she'd smiled. He'd never held a girl quite like her. No other girl could feel the same inside his arms, a cup and saucer that fit perfectly together.

But right now, things didn't look good. North of the crossing, he turned right onto La Veta and trudged eastward toward Orange. Above the floodline, on dry ground, he could walk faster. He angled north. He jogged Glassell around the circle past the unlit Watson's Drug Store. Sunlight was prying through dark clouds again, but rain continued soaking through his hair. He covered up his forehead with his ballcap.

The bill on Willie's Hollywood Stars baseball cap was drenched but kept the rain out of his eyes. Willie sprinted north. He reached the Orange-Olive Road that paralleled the soggy ballast of the old Santa Fe roadbed, too waterlogged to carry trains.

The ground looked dry up near the tracks. He scrambled onto the embankment.

From the top, he saw the Santa Ana River.

Then his heart stopped. Half the town of Olive was submerged. Any bridges that had crossed the Santa Ana were washed out. Cars were flipped onto their sides. Floods had pushed them into piles like in junkyards. Homes knocked off concrete foundations were collapsing. One was floating down the Santa Ana River. Timbers spiraled toward the ocean in a silent sea of flotsam.

Willie shuddered. A week ago, someone had slept inside that house. And Elena hadn't lived inside a house but in a *barn.*

He panicked. If the little town of Olive wasn't here, and if Elena lived in Atwood, another mile up the river in an *outbuilding* a farmer rented out to her *abuelo....*

Willie was afraid to even think about it.

But the torrent had slowed down. He could almost *swim* the river, something he dreaded. He'd had nightmares about drowning all his life. He placed the watch into his baseball cap and crammed it onto his head. He waded out into the current. It was swimmable, but wide. And it was cold. Swirling waters splashed his workshirt and his chin. Willie could breaststroke. He dove in, holding his head above the water, keeping the watch dry.

He drifted with the current.

It was tough swimming with shoes. He kicked them off into the river. They floated south into the turbulence as Willie frog-kicked hard toward the north riverbank. His arms ached. But just thinking of Elena kept him moving. Kept him warm. The mud-caked northern shore approached.

He collapsed onto the bank beside a muddy field of oranges east of Anaheim. He took his shirt off, wrung it out and then replaced it. Mangled rails from the railroad tracks rose up from the river where a bridge had been demolished by the floods.

The rails continued north to Atwood. Now all Willie had to do was make his way along the train tracks or the riverbank to Atwood using the Santa Ana River and the rails as his compass. Barefoot, he trudged upstream through fields of valencias, east along the river toward the Mexican encampments where Elena and the farmworkers had lived outside the orchards.

He walked two miles. There were pricklies in the groves. They hurt his feet, except the soil was so wet they weren't as nasty as they could be. After an hour, he followed train tracks and Placentia-Yorba Boulevard a mile to the Richfield Road stop sign.

Where was Atwood?

Willie looked around.

Nothing was here.

His jaw dropped, and his heart sank. Cadillacs were parked aslant up on the hillsides. But piled up Model T's were ploughed into the mudbanks where the bridges used to be. The Atwood train station was gone. All the outbuildings and barns had disapperared.

They'd washed away beneath the floods roaring through Santa Ana Canyon, powered by massive mountain watersheds upstream.

Where was Elena or her barn? Where was that military stove she used to cook on? Where were all the other buildings and her abuelo? *Jesus Christmas, where was Atwood?*

Half the town was underwater, and the other half was....

Willie gave a shudder.

It was gone!

He felt heartsick and too stunned to even breathe in the cold air. He knew *no one* up here, miles north of home and Santa Ana. Everyone had disappeared, driven out by all the floods.

He swallowed hard. There was the house up on the hilltop where that farmer lived, who used to own the barn Elena lived in.

Willie had no choice but visit him. He trudged up the dirt driveway walking barefoot like a pauper. He pulled the ballcap off his head and checked his watch. It had a dial Elena said looked like a compass. *Quarter-to-eight*. He was glad the watch still worked but felt the bill fall off the baseball cap and plop onto the mud.

Shaking his head, he stumbled forward. He still had to find Elena.

Willie kicked the cap into the muck.

Willie made his way uphill, beyond a copse of tilted mailboxes to a yellow clapboard farmhouse off Placentia-Yorba Boulevard. The Santa Fe tracks that had led him here had functioned as a levee, directing the Santa Ana River toward the south side of the railbed. Within its floodway, the Mexican encampments were destroyed. The rich people lived higher up the hill and still had homes. Oil wells and nodding donkeys lined their Yorba Linda foothills where the Richfield Oil Field wells were still extracting money.

It all seemed so unfair. There'd been a dam proposed upstream to stop the floods, except the Prado Dam had yet to be constucted. Clearly the Feds were not concerned how many people died downstream. They were just migrants who had perished, and nobody seemed to mind.

He slicked his hair back into place. Wiped the mud caked on his feet onto a doormat that informed him he was calling on "The Nortons". He tucked his shirt in, rolled down his trousers. No point in looking like a hobo who would never get respect. He needed help to find Elena.

Porch light was on. He rang the doorbell. Checked his watch. Just shy of eight. Willie hoped someone might answer. Lights were on inside the kitchen. He waited. Watched the second hand go twice around the dial. *Eight o'clock.*

A bolt slid. Someone cracked open the door.

A slim woman in a farm dress with anger etched into her wrinkles glared at Willie. Her six-inch chain bolt blocked the threshold. She looked livid.

"Who are you?" She smoked a Parliament. The pack was in her hand. She exhaled in his face.

Willie stepped back.

Behind the door the stranger glowered at Willie.

A man behind her racked a shotgun, making certain Willie heard it. Guy looked scared. Pointed both barrels of the shotgun straight at Willie.

Willie stammered. "I'm so sorry, I'm, uh...." Willie took a breath. "I'm out here looking for a flood victim."

"We look like victims to you, boy?" The lanky woman cocked

her head and rubbed her pack of cigarettes until some cellophane peeled off onto the rag rug on the floor.

"They used to live out in your barn."

"We have no barn."

"Before the flood."

She gave Willie a look that could freeze hellfire, took a long draw off her cigarette and frowned.

The man holding the shotgun didn't move.

"Just south, there used to be a barn. Elena lived there with her grandfather."

"There was no barn. There never...."

"What?"

"There never was no lousy barn down there." The old man with the shotgun interrupted, nostrils flaring. "Go away. We never rented out them barns. They were fer...."

"Liar." Willie crammed his foot into the opening. "Yes. You did."

"Never had tenants. Never will. Don't care for half-breeds. Never did."

"Except, I'm Irish."

"You and Anthony Quinn both," the woman snorted. "Hollywood swears on it. But any smart person can see it in your eyes. Mexican blood."

"Well I'm American. Born right here in Santa Ana," Willie said, fearing he didn't feel as certain as he sounded.

These people lied right through their teeth. And they looked scared to tell the truth. "And don't come back, ever again. Ya hear me, boy? We don't like half-breeds." The woman blew her cigarette breath straight at Willie.

He stepped back.

Felt the door slam in his face.

Half-breed? What in Hades? A lot of Irish had dark features. He'd read his people were in Ireland before the Celt invasion. Even his father had dark features. Told his friends he was "black Irish."

Cold bone-numbing gusts blew west from Santa Ana Canyon.

Their chill froze Willie in the dark outside a town that wasn't here, that never was here, evidently, although Willie could recall it like the backside of his hand. No one would speak about Elena. Couldn't somebody just come up with the truth?

A blink of lightning.

Except there was no truth in Atwood anymore. There was no Atwood.

A crash of thunder.

A big live oak swayed in the wind on an embankment past the orchards.

Willie rubbed his weary eyes.

Two brighter flashes. Louder rumbling. It was too dangerous to make his way back home. He was exhausted. He'd need to sleep beneath that oak tree up the slope beyond the orange groves. The oak could shelter him from rain. He said a prayer any new lightning struck the tree and not himself and that its branches didn't fall down in the rain.

CHAPTER II

SANTA ANA: SATURDAY, MARCH 5

It was as if the recent storms had washed the Mexicans away. Had even washed away the memories that migrants had existed. Everyone was in denial or in no-win situations. No one wanted to admit they might have rented out to Mexicans, and everyone seemed terrified some do-gooder attorney might sue their pants off if the word got out some tenants might have drowned.

It took four hours to walk home with all the trolleys out of service. When there were no cars on the highways, it was difficult to hitchhike. Frightened locals whispered hobos had been flushed from their encampments. But no survivors he encountered looked like Mexican *obreros* Willie might question to find out about Elena.

At last, he made his way down Tenth Street, half a block away from Mildred's place. He hadn't learned a thing about

Elena up in Atwood. Three men had told him he was crazy. "There were no wetbacks. End of story." Sounded so certain he had wanted to believe them and go home. Except he *knew* it was a lie. He could still taste Elena's kiss, last time he'd seen her in her cotton dress she'd sewn with her own hands, her flirty smile and her laugh, the way wild butterflies would follow her, like magic, the way she held him like she wished their warm embrace might last forever.

But it hadn't.

Straight ahead was Mildred's house.

He swallowed. He couldn't stand that shoe-faced shrew. She soured his stomach. He wished he had another mile to walk before he faced her.

He wiped the mud from his bare feet, climbed the porch steps, turned the doorknob. It was locked. Pop wasn't home. He heard Mildred in the kitchen.

Willie knocked.

She didn't answer.

Pacing, Willie waited, piqued that Mildred let him stand out in the rain in his bare feet. He held his temper. It wasn't Mildred's fault he hadn't found Elena.

But it seemed Mildred was even more annoyed than Willie.

Yes, he'd left without permission. He'd been scared about Elena. He was *still* worried. It was pointless telling Mildred about that. This was *her* house. She reminded Pop at every opportunity. Willie spied her through the door glass. She was carrying a suitcase. *His* suitcase. She set it down and unlocked the front door.

Willie swallowed extra hard.

Mildred smiled and cleared her throat.

"We need to have a little chat, Willie." Her cheery tone gave Willie nausea. It was that tone she usually saved for when she'd won a round of hearts. It set Willie's nerves on red alert. "I've done a little research, and...."

"Where's Pop?"

"It's not important. What is important...," she smiled, inviting him inside, "...is in this envelope. I suggest that you sit down."

Willie stepped back.

Mildred flashed the sort of smile he used to see when cops were apprehending bootleggers on newsreels.

His heart cranked into overdrive.

Stepping inside, her home felt colder than the inside of those ice boxes at Sears. Pop was gone. Something was up. With Willie's suitcase by the front door it was clear Mildred had some sort of agenda up her sleeve. Willie braced himself.

She gave the envelope to Willie.

It was nine by twelve, manila, with a string around the clasp that took a minute to unravel. Everything about the moment seemed bizarre. Willie reached inside the envelope. He found a slip of paper from the Orange County Courthouse. A birth certificate.

He read it:

CERTIFICATE OF BIRTH
Guillermo Juan O'Toole
Sex – M
Born 3:15 A.M. January 4th 1919
Santa Ana, California
Mother: Maria Juana O'Toole
Father: undisclosed
Race – Mexican.

Mexican? He wasn't Mexican but Irish. Pop had said so. The last time he'd been called Mexican, he'd punched that sucker out his junior year behind the tennis court at Santa Ana High. A darned shame he couldn't do the same to Mildred.

His breath fled. He felt dizzy. He fought to appear calm and cover up emotions crawling all around his head. He was at least three-quarters Irish. *Wasn't O'Toole an Irish name?*

"What is this, Mildred?" Willie's hands were shaking harder than an air hammer.

"A certificate of birth."

"I know, Mildred. But whose?"

"I think you know, Willie." She said it with such coldness Willie almost felt the frost but didn't see it on the windows.

"Is this...?"

"Your mother?"

"How 'bout Pop?"

"I'm afraid he's not your father." Mildred shrugged as if she'd just informed him water could be wet.

"Not my father?" Willie's heart stopped.

"Never was, honey. I found this on your birthday at the courthouse. Stanley implored me not to tell you. He likes to keep up the charade. But I no longer see the point. When I asked you to remain with us and guard my place from looters, you made it clear that your priorities weren't with us."

So that was it. Words unfit to speak swirled through his mind. But it seemed Mildred's rage was just getting warmed up.

"Willie, your mother was a whore."

A flash of anger seared his brow. "A bit of nerve you have. You really shouldn't speak ill of the dead." He glared at Mildred. Raised his hand, but he restrained himself from slapping her.

"Just being honest." Mildred shrugged. "Are you so sure your mother died?"

"Pop said so." Willie slammed his palm against the door jamb. Rubbed his hand. Mildred's words had stung him harder than her doorframe.

"You weren't even Stanley's baby, even if he raised you like you were. He came home drunk and spilled the beans to me on more than one occasion. He had this friend. Miguel O'Reilly used to show up from Chihuahua. A dark-skinned Irishman whose grandfather had been a San Patricio. I looked them up. They were deserters who, in eighteen-forty-six, committed treason. Joined the Mexicans and fought against our country. This man Miguel shows up and knocks up Stanley's girlfriend, then skips town. So Stanley raised you as his own. The man's a bleeding heart, a do-gooder. It's almost like he thinks it makes him Christian."

"Stuff it, Mildred." Willie paused to take a breath and recollect himself. He shuddered. He'd need to get a grip on his emotions. But what was he supposed to think when his whole life people had said he was American? It seemed neither of his parents had been born here. Worse, the white side of his family had been traitors.

"Willie, you're just like them. You *deserted* us," said Mildred." We needed you to help defend my house after the flood." She straightened herself. She always wore her pumps to appear taller. "Willie, you can't run from the truth. Sooner or later it will find you. You've been dodging it for years, and it's high time somebody told you."

"So, where did Pop go?"

"I told him that he might not want to be here when...."

"You threw his son out on the street."

"You're not *his* son. You're Miguel's."

She crossed her arms and shrugged again, shaking those ugly ash-blond curls from off her cheeks onto her shoulders.

"And you call yourself a Christian?"

"Oh, be a man. You *are* nineteen."

"I don't believe this." Willie balled his fists and shook his head. *Best to stay calm*. He might say something he regretted. Or explode. A bad idea if he knew Mildred. She'd go straight to the police.

Mildred handed Willie his old suitcase.

She pointed toward Tenth Street. "*Au revoir*, Willie," she whispered.

He grabbed the handle. "Goodbye, Mildred. It's been swell. Thanks for the memories."

"Toodle-loo." Her voice was sweet enough to make a fellow's ears bleed, and all those sharp and shiny teeth looked like a buzzsaw.

Willie turned, hoisted his suitcase. He made his way out the front door and down the steps. He started whistling to chase away his fury. From *Snow* White: Whistle While You Work. It made Willie think of witches and their apples.

The door shut in the bungalow behind him.

He set his chin and soldiered on in his bare feet with his old suitcase. He wished that he could spit, but that would just make him look weak. Weakness was a luxury a man could not afford in this Depression. He would need to find a way.

One silver lining. Noone could stop him now from searching for Elena.

The rain dripped from his hair into his eyes.

CHAPTER III

SATURDAY, MARCH 5

Willie thought if there was any place he might run into Pop, it was either at Hub's Tavern or downtown at Clark-Dye Hardware. After rifling through his suitcase, he laced on old Buster Browns he had outgrown. Willie made his way down Fifth Street toward Downtown.

The too-tight shoes pinched on his feet, raising raw blisters on his toes. But what blistered even worse was the way Pop hadn't stood up for him. He'd thought the old man cared about him. Now he felt conflicted. *Fat chance.* The old man only cared for Mildred and cheap whiskey.

All hotels downtown were full. Thanks to the floods, there were no rooms. Even the Hotel Santa Ana's neon sign spelled out "NO VACANCY." Not that it mattered. It was like Willie wore a sign that said, "NO MONEY." He'd saved up eighty-seven dollars, but Saturdays his bank was closed.

Four girls played hopscotch on the sidewalk. Willie made his way around them. Saw the hardware store. He peered in through the window. There was Pop, behind the ladders. It was clear he'd had some drinks. He wasn't walking straight but didn't seem aware that he was sozzled.

Willie straightened. Marched inside, feeling his temples drum with fury. All these years he had been treated like an outcast. Now he knew why.

Inside the door, he set his suitcase down. He beelined toward the paint section where Stanley read the label on a can of Dutch Boy Paint.

Willie smacked his palm and cleared his throat.

Pop glanced up. He flashed Willie a stunned look and backed away.

Willie stepped forward. "We need to have a little talk, Stan, but you're drunk." Willie's fists felt like two wrecking balls that dangled from his arms.

The old man raised his chin, and then he staggered two steps back. "Willie, what'sh up?" He rubbed his knuckles like he did when he was nervous.

"I think you know." Willie's fist pounded his palm so hard it felt like he had bruised it in a fight he'd never had.

The old man grinned through crooked teeth the color of canned corn. His head was shaking. He was sweating. Then he stammered. "Shit. You saw Mildred?"

Willie glared at him. "Good guess."

"I meant to tell you."

"Sure, you did."

"Why did that woman...?" The old man steadied himself, reeling, almost knocking over paint cans.

"It's her house. You know the rules as well as I do."

Pop glanced away.

Willie was trying to stay calm. "And when I needed you, you split, you hen-pecked coward, letting your girlfriend wear the pants while you get pickled. I just got tossed out like the trash after I paid the rent through March so I can sleep in a garage that's now a full foot underwater. I have *no* respect for *you*, Stan." Willie's voice cracked. He took a deep breath. "Zero." He made a zero with his thumb and index finger and shot a glance over his shoulder.

Customers stared his direction.

His gut was swimming with emotion. Memories were carouselling like some old forgotten newsreel. In it, he longed to see his mother. Those nights the old man came home drunk, and he'd punch Willie in the face, nights he'd wished there might be somebody to tuck him into bed, tell him a story like the real boys got to hear in real houses.

"I can exshplain, son."

Willie breathed in. Tightened his jaw. "Don't you ever call me *son*." He crossed his arms. "Mildred just spilled all the beans. Says Mom's alive."

"Your mother's dead, Willie."

"LIAR!"

The old man took a swing at Willie. Missed.

He swung again, connecting this time with a hard jab to the jaw that rattled Willie. Another gut punch. A left hook toward his ear.

Ducking, Willie caught his fist. Bent back the wrist.

The old man shrieked.

"My real father," Willie whispered. "Who's my father?"

"I-I don't know."

"Where's my mother? Did she run off with her lover?"

"Who gives a damn, Willie? I don't. I stopped Mary June from killing you. She had tickets for the bus to TiaJuana. To abort you."

Willie froze. He'd never heard that. "Liar, you told me she was dead. Seconds ago."

"No. I didn't."

"You really think that I'm that stupid?"

Willie's spine felt like an icicle. "I'm sick and tired of all your lousy contradictions. Gimme the truth for once." He bent back the wrist so hard the old man winced.

"Okay, okay. I had to marry her to shtop her."

"Well how did that work out?" snapped Willie, fearing he sounded too sarcastic. Time to dial down his temper. Be the adult if no one else would.

Time stood still. He looked around.

He sucked in a deep breath.

Somebody was looking his direction.

His temples pulsed like Chick Webb's snare drum on the radio when he stomped at the Savoy. Gene Krupa hammered on the other temple, pounding even faster.

Crowds gathered around like Pop and Willie were in the ring, and all the locals in their overalls had paid to see a fight.

"Mary June left when you were five."

"She didn't die, then."

"She died later."

"How do *you* know?"

"Got a letter."

"My dead mother writes you letters?"

"Don't be a shmarty-pants."

"A what? Don't be a liar. I got evidence. From Mildred. A birth certificate. Says my real name's Guillermo."

"Mildred *what?*" Stanley's eyes enlarged. They looked like two alarm bells. He was wobbling, the booze plus the exertion from the fight.

Willie glared at him. "You lied to me. For years."

The old man stood his ground. "For your own good, Willie."

"For *my* good? Are you expecting me to thank you?" He couldn't stop shaking his head. It made no sense.

Stan raised his fist again to throw another punch.

Willie dodged, then shoved him hard into the row of Dutch Boy paint cans stacked up high between two aisles. Gallon cans rolled all directions across brown and green linoleum. Pop grabbed his elbow where he'd fallen. A can of paint had busted open, bleeding orange across Stan's brown lumberjack shirt.

Stooping, Willie pressed a knee against Stan's chest and leaned down hard. "I'm only gonna ask you one more time."

Stan glared back up at him. "I shtill don't know. But he was...."

"Mexican? You always told me I was Irish." Willie frowned." Finally admitting that you lied?" Willie leaned back.

"*He* was Irish. Irish-Mexican. What the hell difference does it make?"

"He wasn't born here. Mildred tells me I'm descended from deserters. San Patricios or some darn thing"

"In Mexico, they're heroes."

"We aren't in Mexico," said Willie. "And up here they call it treason. People hang for it, especially if they don't even belong here."

"Willie, no one's gonna hang you."

"Where am I supposed to go? Who's gonna hire me if my birth certificate calls me a Mexican?"

"One-quarter Mexican. Miguel was Irish. Your Ma was half-Irish half-Yaqui. You're not so dark you couldn't pass yourself. Tell people you're a dago."

"Doesn't matter. My face can be as white as Crisco. I'm still a greaser. A half-breed *cholo*. People say that's even worse."

"Shpare me the pity party. How would it help to tell the truth? It ain't helpful. Don't you get it? You need to keep the mashquerade up if you're shmart. Or did your gal forget to tell you Mexicans can get deported? Nothin' wrong with 'em. They work their bloody tails off like serfs. But there ain't no one saying *gracias* up here. People are hungry, and the Mexicans are taking away jobs."

Willie rose to let a stockboy with a dust bin and a mop sponge up the puddle of orange paint from the linoleum. Pop was straddled among paint cans. Paint seeped though the old man's trousers. His shoes and all his clothing had been ruined.

The stockboy brought a can of turpentine and scrubbed the tile clean.

The old man stumbled back onto his feet.

He glared at Willie, hands on his hips, shaking his head, his face contorted. "All I can tell you is shove off, you lousy ingrate. After everything...Oh, crap."

Here came the store owner." Both you guys. Outta here." He jerked a nail-less thumb over his shoulder." I said, scram. Lickety-split outta my store. We've had enough trouble already with the floods. I don't need more. If you two amateur Joe Louis's ain't gone before I find myself a phone, I'm gonna call in the police."

"I shoulda dumped you off at County." Stanley glared at Willie. Spit. "For all the thanks I gets."

Willie about-faced. No point in arguing with drunks. He had enough trouble already, and he needed to find work. He made his way toward the door, marching in quick time. Grabbed the suitcase.

"Willie, you ruin my new trousers. Anger my lady friend. And now?"

"You're the one who threw the punches."

"Now I can't even show my face in here. Go screw yourself. You lousy no-good *cholo*. Find Elena. Find...a job."

"I *have* a job."

"Not bussing tables at some taco stand." He wagged his finger like the nuns at Saint Anne's Catholic Church on Main Street. "Know what your problem is, Willie?" Pop shook a fist. "You think life's fair. Well it's a hustle. Every palooka's got an angle. You ain't owed shquat."

Willie kept walking, and Pop's voice faded behind him.

"So, shut your yap. Go find a job. Shomeday, you'll thank me."

Willie shook his head.

The poor old man had looked pathetic in that paint aisle and still did. But he'd never treated Willie well and hit him all the time. Willie had never punched him back, he thought. And that took some control. Maybe he was a lousy ingrate, but it didn't matter now that they had thrown him onto the street when he'd already paid the rent.

Willie glanced back. But now he didn't say a word. He'd find a hustle. No thanks to Stanley there, or Mildred, or his dead-or-alive mother. Somehow, he'd have to find Elena. She was the one person who made him feel strong.

Willie picked up the pace.

Didn't look back.

He had a job at Josefina's bussing tables.

Willie glanced down at his wristwatch.

Four-fifteen. He'd need to hurry. His paces became quicker. It gladdened him the rain had finally stopped.

So according to his birth certificate, he was a Mexican, even though he'd heard only a quarter of him was. But even Mrs. Norton had picked up on it in Atwood. Dark brown eyes, proof enough he wasn't 100-percent white. Not to mention a complexion one might call "Mediterranean." Mildred saw it. He'd been fooling himself. Everybody saw it. He was a fake, a fraud, a phony trying to pass as a Caucasian, a mutt trying to pretend he was some purebred with a pedigree like Mildred's, when he belonged down at the pound.

Plus, Willie had another problem, even though he had a job. He needed someplace he could stay since he'd been thrown out on the streets, which still hadn't been swept free of the debris left from the storms. Willie struggled west on Fifth Street.

He lugged his heavy suitcase, switching arms after two blocks. Cramps knotted his neck. Time to stop to catch his breath. Blisters stung his feet. But there was no point being angry. There were names for folks like Mildred. A part of Willie hoped he'd never see that witch again. The old man had disappointed him. Sad how the Depression had emasculated Stanley. Willie had looked up to him. All of that had changed within two hours. Willie was comforted the man bore no relation.

Then he recalled both of his parents had deserted him as well. Even his parents were ashamed of him and hadn't stuck around.

But that was life in the big city, or the big town of Santa Ana, population 30,000 and the seat of Orange County, or what remained of it after record-breaking floods had scoured through town. His steps quickened. He had hoped to be at work a little early.

There were so many things it seemed Willie O'Toole had just shrugged off until today, such as how people sometimes labeled him as "Spanish," the local euphemism for Mexicans who happened to speak English. It was making perfect sense as Willie made his way toward work.

Why he'd been hired at Josefina's having the only Irish surname, why he'd connected with Elena, why he'd never felt at home living at Mildred's. He'd been denying it, but now it fit together, memories of his mother singing songs and telling tales of *La Llorona* drowning two sons in the Santa Ana River after their father had deserted her. Then *La Llorona* had drowned *herself*, perhaps why nightmares about drowning had been troubling him for years.

Still he'd swam across the Santa Ana River for Elena. She had this way of making Willie feel brave the way his mother had. He'd adored his mother. Then she'd disappeared like *La Llorona*. He remembered how she smelled, the scent of *masa* on her hands when she had hugged him. Her charming smile like Elena's that had warmed his very soul. But like a fire that goes out on a dark night, Willie now shivered, and the hole inside his heart sucked in the cold.

Fresh scents of cornstarch were a quarter block ahead at Josefinas. The smell reminded Willie of his mother even now. It was part of why he liked it there, besides the fact they'd offered him a job in the Depression. They always made him feel at home, something he needed even more since he'd been thrown out on his own.

Willie stopped at the new mural on the wall of Josefina's. A girl painted on the masonry bore Elena's spitting image. *But how could that be?* His jaw dropped. Surely Elena never came here. Her home was in that barn with her *abuelo* up in Atwood.

The sun glared from the west into Willie's weary eyes.

He took a hard gulp and remembered. Set his jaw and swallowed tears. Hard to think about Elena's disappearance. Like his mother, he had no clue where to find her, had no proof she had survived. He breathed in deep. Once he got back onto his feet he would find out.

It was time to go to work.

He made his way up concrete steps. Willie's blistered feet were throbbing.

Josefina turned toward Willie. She wore a black polka-dot blouse over gray slacks. She waved hello. *"Parece triste.* Why so sad?"

"Long story," muttered Willie. Then he pointed toward the mural. *"Esa chica."* He looked at Josefina. *"¿Quién es ella?"*

"Why, *es Loretta, mi vecina.* Comes here Saturdays for supper. Her boyfriend, Rico, he drives that thirty-seven Auburn," Fina whispered.

"They come often?"

"Every month. Not so often for her friend."

Willie studied the maroon car parked on Fifth Street, an Auburn boat-tail convertible, the sort of car driven by movie stars and gangsters. Willie's mind was piqued with curiosity. What was an Auburn boat-tail speedster doing here in Santa Ana just a day after the record-breaking floods?

Nobody local drove an Auburn. Auburn stopped making those in 1937.

He glanced back up at the mural, and the image of Elena. Then, he looked down at his watch. *Four-fifty-eight.* He shut his eyes.

It was time to go inside and get to work bussing their tables, washing dishes.

The scent of *masa* warmed his heart, and he embraced it.

He liked it here. At times he even thought he was at home. He made his way inside the shop, telling himself after his shift he'd need to find a local park bench where he'd catch up on some sleep.

But for three and one-half hours he had to work.

CHAPTER IV

SATURDAY, MARCH 5

The screen door slammed behind him. The lines behind the counter inside Josefina's dining room were sparse after the floods. Juan was scribbling down the orders at the register tonight. His grown-up daughter, Josefina, brought a tray of fresh *tamales* to a couple who were drinking at a table in the corner.

Willie's jaw fell. *Was that Loretta?* Her face looked like Elena's, hair pulled tight in a barette above Elena's dark brown eyes. She was his girlfriend's spitting image, except she'd spent more on her threads, a store-bought dress Willie had seen downtown at Buffums in their windows on those mannequins who always had their noses in the air.

A slim man in a tan suit and fedora sat across from her. He looked to be from out of town. He lit Loretta's cigarette. She inhaled and looked away. Then her gaze landed on Willie. She was staring at him. Riveted. He couldn't help but notice.

Willie had to turn aside. It was almost like she recognized him. Willie backed away.

Loretta's escort tapped his water glass, asked Willie for a refill.

Willie hurried into the kitchen. Found a pitcher. Added one big scoop of ice and made his way back toward the dining room.

He refilled both their glasses with cold water.

That woman had to be Loretta. The face could be Elena's, but with makeup and hoop earrings large enough to seat canaries. Her gaze was glued to Willie's wristwatch. She touched his forearm. Said, "*Perdon*."

Willie drew his arm back. *Those eyes looked almost like Elena's.*

She kept staring at him, stroking on her chin with her free hand.

The tan-suit stranger turned toward Willie. "*Su reloj*." He drummed the table with his fingernails. *¿Dónde está de? A mi amiga aquí le gustaría saberlo, por favor*."

They were addressing him in Spanish. The man was clearly European, unlike Loretta, puffing her Marlboro across from him and frowning. Perhaps the stranger came from Italy.

"My watch?"

"*¿Habla Ingles, boy?*"

"I was born here," Willie mumbled.

"I apologize," the gentleman replied. "My lady friend here, she would like to know about your wristwatch."

Loretta's gaze made Willie nervous. It left him feeling like he'd stolen it.

Willie sucked his cheeks in. Grinned. "My girlfriend gave it to me."

"*Que bueno.*" Loretta deadpanned, brown eyes riveted to Willie's. "*¿Como se llama?*" She removed a paper tissue from her purse.

Willie shrugged and said, "Elena Valenzuela."

Loretta's face froze.

Her cigarette wagged in her hand. She exhaled a plume of smoke, brought her Kleenex to her lip and dabbed her lipstick. Willie knew he'd struck a nerve.

"*¿Esa Elena. A donde vive?*" The woman's gaze could drill through brick.

"Atwood." Willie mopped his brow. "Before the rains."

Loretta's face turned even whiter. She froze as if the blood inside her veins had turned to ice. She snuffed her Marlboro out in her tin ashtray. She had smoked less than an inch of it. She whirled to face her escort. Grabbed her purse and rose to leave. "*Enrico, vámonos.*" She snapped her fingers, and he rose, marionette-like.

"But we just got here, kitten."

Loretta didn't speak another word. She stormed outside, dabbing mascara with her wadded paper napkin. Willie had no clue exactly what had set her off.

Enrico followed. Shaking his head, he left a Lincoln on the table and rushed out, calling Loretta's name behind her through the doorway. Willie heard the Auburn screech away. Through metal window blinds, he noticed there was no one in the car beside Enrico.

But after matters had calmed down, Willie couldn't help but overhear the gossip over "Tight-Sweater Loretta" dashing out. Everybody had a theory on why she'd stormed outside.

It seemed none of them made any sense at all.

The last person that Willie had expected to encounter as he walked out of the restaurant was Tight-Sweater Loretta. She'd changed her clothes. She must live close if she was Josefina's neighbor. It was immediately clear why men had given her the moniker.

Her flame-red sweater appeared custom-made to showcase all her assets. Willie had to look away. She had the same face as Elena's, but Elena hid her figure while Loretta showed hers off. They could be twins, so alike, and yet, in many ways, so different.

She stared again at Willie's wristwatch, looking more jaded than before. She lit a Marlboro. Puffed it. "So, what's the story, mornin' glory?" The shadow from a streetlight cast a twenty-foot-long stripe running down Fifth Street. Loretta's other hand was jammed against her hip.

Nervous, Willie backed away. "Excuse me, madam?"

Loretta pointed to his suitcase. "Looks like you need a place to stay." She puffed her cigarette without batting an eyelash. Looked away. Glared back at Willie, as if daring him to answer.

But he didn't.

"Josefina said the floods caused you some trouble."

"I was evicted,"

"Kid, you're in luck," Loretta said. "I got a guest room. Only fifty cents a night. In your case, forty."

"Why the bargain?" Willie frowned.

Loretta pointed down the sidewalk with her cigarette. She smiled.

"Josefina says nice things about you, Willie. And besides, you know Elena."

"Used to know her," Willie said, tilting his head. He had his doubts about this woman.

"Little birdie said Elena was your doll." Loretta's chin cocked at an angle. Her hips swiveled on long legs atop her pumps in a provoking sort of way.

"Floods washed her out." Willie's hands balled into fists. He couldn't look her in the eye. "Spent a day searching for her. Came up with no clue on where she went."

Loretta stared off into space. "You and me both, kid." A gentle sigh.

"You two related?" Willie asked. "Elena said she had two sisters. You two look astoundingly alike."

Loretta's Mona Lisa smile seemed to telegraph she wasn't up for sharing. "Close enough. Too bad Enrico doesn't think so. Let's get some rest. You sound exhausted."

"But I can't pay you now. My cash is in the bank."

"First week is free, so grab your grip, Willie. I'm half a block away. Not safe to sleep out on the street."

"But..."

"No excuses." Loretta waved her cigarette and started walking.

"W-what would Rico say?"

"He isn't who you think he is."

"Yeah, right."

"We're strictly business partners."

"Sure."

"And nothing more." Loretta voice wavered.

Then like a dragon in high heels, Loretta blew a puff of smoke and marched down the sidewalk toward her house, high heels clicking on slick concrete. "Coming, Willie?"

He shivered, swallowed hard, and bit his nerves back. "What the heck."

He followed several steps behind her, dodging piles of debris left on the sidewalks by the floods. Moonlight reflected on wet walkways. He lugged his suitcase up red Spanish-tile steps toward a brown and yellow bungalow on Olive Street.

He wasn't quite sure what to make of it. The yard was full of prickly pears and *chollas* plus a bathtub Virgin Mary by the driveway. He was surprised to see no weeds, especially after all the floods, like someone stopped by every day to tidy up for the Madonna. They'd left one castor bean plant thriving in a corner by the hose bibb as if a gardener had believed it was a private marijuana bush and didn't know those little beans could kill you if you ate them.

Willie set the suitcase on the steps.

He shook his arm out.

Loretta unlocked an arched door that was the color of the roof tile.

Willie followed her inside into a white plaster interior with absolutely nothing on the walls.

"Well, this is it." Loretta led him to a guest room down her hallway. Turned the light on. "*Buenas noches.*" She had the soft voice of a torch singer, like Elena's except raspier, perhaps because she smoked.

"*Hasta mañana,*" Willie muttered.

Loretta shut the door behind her.

Willie sat down on the bed. Kicked off his bloody Buster Browns. Rolled off his socks. His feet were swollen and had silver-dollar blisters. He told himself on Monday he would buy some shoes that fit.

He thought of Mildred. Fought back anger.

Thought of Stanley. Fought back pity.

Thought of Elena. Recalled her smile. Touched his watch.

Bent over. Wept.

CHAPTER V

SUNDAY, MARCH 6

Willie awoke to banging church bells from Saint Anne's Catholic Church ten blocks away from him on Main Street. He threw his undershirt and pants on. He made his way into a kitchen lined with olive-green wood shelves cluttered with rusty iron skillets, eclectic cereal-box glassware, and salt and pepper shakers painted up like cute ceramic toys from every tourist trap in Southern California.

A pot of Chase and Sanborn coffee percolated in the corner. Loretta was seated at her kitchen table, sucking on her cigarette. She wore the sweater from last night over a pair of dirty Levis and a necklace made from corn, the sort they sell in TiaJuana. A dozen Marlboro butts filled a green metallic ashtray, the ivory-tip ends slathered with her lipstick. She was staring at a wall clock. It looked every bit as boring as those clocks in public schools, except it seemed to entertain her.

"*Café,* Willie?" She glanced up. Loretta pointed to the pot. The aroma filled the kitchen. "It's fresh. Made it myself."

Willie found a cup and saucer that said, "Catalina Island." He rinsed its silverfish and dust into the sink and poured some coffee. He took a sip and saw Loretta had stopped staring at the wall clock. She studied him and set her cigarette down.

"Willie, you're not wearing your wristwatch."

He met her gaze. "I don't want trouble."

"I'm not trouble. I'm your friend."

"I hardly know you," Willie said.

Loretta eyed him up and down. "I can tell Elena likes you. Very much."

"Liked," said Willie, wishing he'd camouflaged the emphasis he'd placed on the past tense. It left him sounding adolescent.

"You upset, Willie? I just paid you a compliment."

"I heard." He stepped back, letting the steam from his hot beverage shield his face. He took a breath. "What's the big deal about my wristwatch?" Willie asked.

Loretta looked away.

It let him take back the offensive. "Why am I here, ma'am?" Willie asked. "What's your relation to Elena?"

Loretta stared back toward the clock. "Maybe I – like you. Is that wrong?"

"Why am I *really* here, Loretta?" It embarrassed him to finally use her name. He hardly knew her, and he meant to keep his distance. He got the feeling she was using him.

She retrieved her cigarette. Exhaled smoke. Snuffed out the Marlboro and stared toward stumps of palm trees that remained outside her window. At last she pointed to her arm. Loretta's smile disappeared. She pursed her lips, took a deep breath and exhaled. She said, "The wristwatch."

Willie felt a shiver. He took a sip of bitter coffee. Gulped it down. Made a face. "What about it?"

"Elena gave it to you."

"H-how did you know *that?*"

"Honey, I'm brighter than I look. Didn't you tell me just last night, or were you lying?"

He had told the truth, but Willie couldn't seem to find his words.

She cleared her throat. "I was hoping you might help me find my – sister."

It was Willie's turn for staring at the clock. Who *was* this woman? Why had she paused, then said Elena was her sister? And they looked so much alike. What did she care about his wristwatch from Elena? She kept staring like she wanted it or something. Well it was *his*. Elena gave it to him. Now that she had vanished, and the rich people in Atwood claimed she'd never ever lived there, it was taking on new meaning, Willie's anchor to reality, reminding him that everyone was lying.

Willie turned to face Loretta. "When did you last hear from Elena?"

"Not recently."

Disappponted, he asked "How recently is recent?"

"Not for a week. She's miles north of here and doesn't have a telephone. Last time I rode up there she said she was in trouble," said Loretta.

"What sort of trouble?"

"She was worried."

"Isn't everybody worried? There's no jobs in Orange County after all the recent floods."

"Jeezus Christmas, do I have to paint a picture?" snapped Loretta. Her glare could freeze a man at twenty paces.

"What are you saying?" He set his coffee down and stared straight at her face. Her dismissive look persuaded him she thought he was naïve.

"Never mind." Loretta picked her cigarette up. Struck a kitchen match, relit it. Blew a smoke ring. "How well do you know Elena?"

Why was this woman so evasive? Willie leaned back in his kitchen chair and told about his trip up to their barn after the flood. How he'd been horrified the barn, the town, Elena, and her grandfather had vanished.

Loretta covered up her mouth and raised her eyebrows.

She set her Marlboro down. Her brown eyes fired at him like bullets. Evidently, something Willie'd said had upset her a lot.

"Why would nobody in Atwood admit Mexicans had lived there?" Willie asked. He rose and paced across the kitchen with his coffee. "Why the lies?"

"She never told you?"

"Who?"

"Elena. Who'd you talk to up in Atwood?"

"Man named Norton."

"Lawrence Norton?" asked Loretta.

"They didn't give me their first names. I read their doormat. And their mailbox. Kept thinking both should say '*pendejos*.'"

Loretta smirked and looked away.

"Norton's wife called me a half-breed. Said she doesn't like our type. Claimed she didn't know Elena Valenzuela. Never did. Claimed she never rents to Mexicans and never had a barn." He slammed his palm down on the metal kitchen table.

"Norton's a bastard and a liar."

"Don't you think I know that?" *Who was this woman? As elusive as the smoke she kept exhaling. But she knew things. Lots of things that Willie didn't have a clue about.*

Loretta met his gaze. "Right now, we need to find Elena."

"And *you* think I can help you?"

Her voice set Willie's nerves on edge, but it heartened him to realize she cared about Elena. "Had much success working alone, Willie?" Her question made his answer obvious. She gestured as if signaling the answer to her question.

He wasn't sure of her agenda but was open to assistance. Working solo he'd found nothing.

"Okay, okay. Where do we start? I looked her name up at the County back in April. Hall of Records makes no mention of Elena."

"But she was born here."

"How do *you* know?"

"She's my – my baby sister? You think the stork brought her?"

"Please don't be sarcastic," Willie said.

"Well for a man who's fully grown you seem alarmingly naïve, if you think any of the *rubios* will care that we exist."

He picked his coffee up and finished the remains with one huge gulp, swished it around like it was mouthwash, spat it out into the sink. "Perhaps I am naïve. So what?"

"Would you just *listen* to me once?"

"All right, okay." Reminded of how Mildred used to treat him, he slammed the cup down by the faucet. "So, I'm listening."

A moth bumped against the kitchen window, trying to fly outside.

Loretta frowned and cocked her head. "You're not full *güero*, but you talk like them."

"Heard of the Irish San Patricios? Fought with General Santa Anna?"

"Your father's side?" Loretta snuffed her Marlboro out against a corner of her ashtray. Grabbed her pack to shake a new one out and frowned.

No cigarettes left.

"Never met him," Willie said. "Lived in Chihuahua."

"And your mother?"

Willie shrugged. "Eight years ago she disappeared."

Loretta drummed her narrow fingers gnawed down to nicotine-beige nails. "You got your dark eyes from your mother, I presume, if Pa was Irish."

"Ma was half-Irish herself."

"Except that other half was..."

"Mexican."

"Exactly." Loretta volunteered a Mona Lisa smirk. "Elena talked about your eyes. I think they're part of why she liked you."

The refrigerator monitor compressor turned on loud enough to rattle the green glassware on the dusty kitchen shelves.

"But to some cops, dark eyes are all the proof they need you're here from Mexico."

"Where else?" A laugh from Willie.

"How about Atwood, California, like Elena. She was born here. Not every person who speaks Spanish is from Mexico."

"Well Orange County has no records of her birth."

Loretta rose. "They like to keep us in the shadows. It's convenient. Makes us easy to look down on." She made her way into the parlor. Retrieved a brown manila envelope from the top drawer of her dresser. Laid a photo on the kitchen table. "Tell me who this is, Willie."

Willie took a hard look at the photo.

It had been taken on the front steps of Saint Boniface Catholic Church in Downtown Anaheim in sepia tones straight out of the Twenties. It surprised Willie the mother could look so much like Elena. Except Elena was the baby. Willie knew those eyes too well. It had to be her in the center in her white embroidered dress bearing a star-encircled image of Our Lady of Guadalupe next to a youngish face of Father Patrick Browne from Dublin, Ireland.

"Any questions," asked Loretta.

Willie choked back grief. "Why do you have this?"

"She's my sister."

"Wouldn't her mother usually keep this?"

"Her mother died."

"Funny, Elena never mentioned that," said Willie, wondering why Elena'd never said a word about her parents and was living in a barn with her *abuelo*.

Loretta frowned. "It isn't something that Elena liked to talk about." Her voice cracked when she'd spoken of Elena in past tense. Loretta grabbed the photo, walked it back into the parlor. She replaced it in the top drawer of her dresser with a slam.

"Okay, so let me get this straight. Your sister's born in California in some barn, so there's no doctor. And the midwife keeps her mouth shut. So the only thing we know is she was baptized up in Anaheim."

"By Father Browne. Go to Saint Boniface. Look it up. It's in their records."

"No, I don't need to. I believe you."

"Finding Elena will be challenging." Loretta poured her half-full cup of coffee down the sink. "We've had no floods like this since 1928 in Santa Paula."

"Saint Francis Dam break?" Willie asked.

Loretta tightened up her face, like she was holding something back, and had to swallow down emotions. She touched a Kleenex to her cheek. "My people camped out by the Santa Clara River in their bedrolls when the waters came and swept them to the sea," Loretta said. "Hundreds of bodies washed ashore outside of Oxnard and Ventura. They had no names. They were just "greasers", and our names weren't in their records. Except to us they were *familia*."

Loretta looked away. "*Como mi madre*." Her expression seemed to harden against sadness.

Willie shuddered. He'd never heard of this and wouldn't have believed it if it wasn't for his heartbreak that Elena'd disappeared. But it made sense if there were people who were living in the shadows of Orange County, or some other county, few people would miss them.

Mildred wouldn't. Nor would Stanley.

Willie met Loretta's gaze and said, "I'll help."

"I was hoping you'd say yes." Loretta smiled and touched his wrist.

He shuddered. Loretta's touch felt like Elena's. Willie turned to face the window. Felt a tear.

Excused himself.

Made his way back to his room.

Shut the door. Turned on the radio.

Loretta hadn't cried.

Neither did Willie.

But it was hours before he felt he could come out.

CHAPTER VI

SATURDAY, MARCH 12

After an uneventful week, he'd made no progress on Elena. Willie dreaded having to reconcile himself with his worst fears. So far, no word from his girlfriend and no word from her *abuelo.* Without them, life just didn't seem the same.

KVOE was on the air again. The "Voice of the Orange Empire" made its way throughout the barbershop on Main Street south of Third. Willie'd stopped to get a haircut from José and read a comic book. A cowbell clattered loudly as a customer departed.

Willie worried about money. He'd withdrawn cash from the bank to buy new shoes, pay Loretta, and deposit a small paycheck. He'd computed his meager funds would disappear within a month. He knew he'd need to find another job.

He paid the barber. The announcer rambled on about the weather and the citrus futures. Prices paid for California oranges had reached stratospheric levels, and a few were making fortunes up near Redlands.

But in Santa Ana, life was pretty grim.

A damn shame losing those orange crops. Farmers had to make a living. Anaheim's Scott-Borden Valencias was going out of business. Life seemed cruel and unfair.

Willie thought about Elena. Every time he was reminded of her, Willie tried to smile.

But every day was getting harder. Then, as he made his way outside, he saw a face a block away that made him freeze.

It was Mildred. She came waltzing out of Buffums with two bags stuffed full of boxes and a pair of purple pumps he'd never seen. Trouble was, in a depression there were people getting wealthy with no effort, while hard-working people struggled to survive.

She swung her purse as she walked toward him. Willie fought to find some words in case she spoke to him. The smacks of her high heels against the sidewalk were as loud as passing motorcars. He smelled Mildred's perfume. It made him nauseous. She didn't even move her tiny eyes.

She marched straight past him in a way that made him think she hadn't seen him. Or didn't want to. Or refused to share the sidewalk with his type. Stanley was probably at work in the Pacific Electric car barns welding steel in the shops to pay for Mildred's champagne tastes.

There were ways of making money. Just not all of them were legal. Willie was pretty sure Loretta had another source of income. He had asked about her partner and his '37 Auburn.

Loretta'd promised she would introduce them.

Today was Saturday. Tonight she met that man at Josefina's. Willie didn't have a clue what Rico did, but he was curious. Not many folks in Santa Ana could afford to drive an Auburn.

Willie couldn't wait to start his shift.

Rico's Auburn was parked across the street from Josefina's. That meant Enrico was inside, probably dining with Loretta. Willie combed his fresh-cut hair and buffed his shoes against his pantlegs. Needing work, he'd need to make a good impression.

Willie made his way inside. Scents of garlic and cilantro filled the dining room. There sat Loretta with Enrico by their window. She wore a fuzzy lime-green sweater and a polka-dotted skirt. She lit her cigarette. She waved. "So what's the deal, banana peel?"

She was looking straight at Willie. "Just told Rico all about you. This is the guy, Rico. Elena's friend."

Enrico didn't move. His face appeared to have been chiseled from a block of solid granite before some joker had crammed a Camel cigarette through rock-hard teeth. He drummed his fingers on the table as if practicing his scales on an invisble piano to a syncopated rhythm. He had a buzz cut, and his cufflinks were the size and shape of dice. "*Si*, Elena's friend." He spoke the words but didn't move his lips. And then he flashed a randy grin that Willie didn't think appropriate. The expression on Loretta's face said Willie was not alone.

Something troubled her. She stared at Rico, eyes like tiny stoplights. Then she flashed a glance at Willie, the sort of look you get when women want protection. But from whom? She'd said Enrico was her partner, and Elena was her sister. Things here didn't quite add up.

But Willie's ears perked up like cats' ears once he heard Elena's name. Nine days of asking everyone in Santa Ana had turned up nothing.

"I'm pleased to meet you, Willie." Enrico wore a tailored woolen suit. He had a soft Italian accent. His brown fedora sat on one side of the table.

He rose to give Willie a handshake that felt weaker than expected. Enrico pulled a wooden chair out. "Care to join us?"

"Help yourself. Hot corn *tortillas* and whipped *mantequilla de ajo*," said Loretta. "Fresh from the kitchen. She gestured toward a scoop of garlic butter.

Willie took a seat. "I was admiring your car," he told Enrico, who didn't answer but massaged his stubbled chin.

Loretta's smile jacked her Marlboro up and down between her teeth. She set her cigarette down. "Rico, tell my friend about the punchboards."

Enrico's eyes flashed back and forth. He fired a glance over his shoulder through the dining room. No people here, except for Josefina, who obligingly departed to the kitchen.

Enrico opened up a patent leather briefcase to his left. It looked old enough to vote, like he had dragged it through a war. He glanced inside and grabbed a punchboard, circus colors, red, blue, and yellow. It said, "Charley Board". Enrico calmly handed it to Willie.

"What's this?" Willie examined a card with foil-covered holes that cost a quarter for one chance to punch one hole and win five-bucks. According to the card there were 170 holes that paid a dollar. Six holes paid five dollars. Willie did the math. If you punched in every hole the card paid out $200, but the chances set you back $250.

"It's a Charlie Board," Enrico said. "You sell it to a merchant for twenty bucks. So Mister Store-owner retains thirty simoleons."

"Isn't that gambling?"

"Sure, it is. But coppers look the other way. It's all in fun. Isn't it, dollface?"

Loretta nodded yes.

"So, what's this got to do with me?" asked Willie.

"I sell you this punchboard for a sawbuck. Ten bucks even, and you flip it to a merchant. Charge him twenty. Bingo-bango. Kid, you just doubled your money. Easy peasy."

"I'm kinda broke, sir. All I got is twenty dollars."

"So, you buy two. Then you come back a after week and buy four more. It's not that hard, kid." Enrico shrugged. His finger tapped against his punchboard.

Loretta snuffed her cigarette out. She shook out another Marlboro.

She bent forward toward Enrico, showing off her ample assets.

He lit her cigarette. The lighter bore his monogrammed initials. It looked to be of solid *gold*. Loretta leaned back in her chair. She sucked her Marlboro, appearing to inhale satisfaction.

Enrico laced his hands behind his head.

"Interested, Willie?" Rico grinned.

Willie's gaze went out the window toward the Auburn by the curbside. Clearly, Rico made good money. Willie could simplify his efforts to find out about Elena if he didn't have to spend so much time working.

Rico leaned back in his chair. His handsome smile seemed to widen like he'd just read Willie's thoughts.

Willie felt a shiver. He looked away. Punchboards were

gambling. They were probably illegal. He looked Mexican. The cops would now arrest him in a heartbeat.

"Almost as good as printing money," Rico's voice punctured the silence. "And I sell hundreds of 'em all over the Southland. Just like candy."

"So, why do you need me?"

"Loretta tells me you speak Spanish. I need market penetration." Enrico shrugged. Met Willie's gaze. "Where the natives don't speak English, kid. *Capisce*? I need a partner."

Willie didn't say a word. He knew his Spanish was pathetic. But he still needed the money, and he liked being called partner. One more glance at Rico's car was all it took.

There was a handshake.

Willie gave the man his twenty.

Enrico gave Willie two Charlie Boards.

And Josefina told him it was time to get to work.

It was that simple.

Loretta grinned at Willie. "*You* owe me a thank you. I must know fifty merchants just in Santa Ana who will buy these."

If it was that easy, he wondered why Loretta wasn't selling them, but clearly, she had other ways of financing her lifestyle.

She stood and headed toward the exit. Waved at Willie and Enrico. "Out the doors, dinosaurs," she said and made her way outside. The sound of her high heels click-click-clicked against the sidewalk. As her footsteps faded off, Willie wondered where she was going. He had suspicions, but he didn't dare to ask.

That night when Willie locked the front door of the bungalow behind him, he found no sign of Loretta, except she'd left on all the lights. He looked around inside her house. She'd clearly stepped out for the night. She'd left a suitcase on the couch half-packed and taken off without it. She didn't drive. Willie suspected she had hopped aboard a Red Car. That meant she wouldn't be returning until sometime in the morning, since the trolleys all stopped running after midnight.

He had yet to find the evidence supporting his suspicion that Loretta made her living as some sort of high-end call girl. Her wardrobe and chain smoking made it clear she made good money. He'd never asked about her livelihood and thought he didn't care. But with no luck finding Elena, Willie now had become desperate. Any clue at all was worth the trouble.

Certain things about this bungalow filled Willie's mind with questions. Like that bathtub Virgin Mary. Loretta wasn't that religious. Someone had harvested her castor beans. The bush had been denuded. There were no pictures on the walls. The vacant rooms, the empty closets; all made Willie think the bungalow belonged to someone else. Tonight, he'd have himself a look around.

He'd be careful. To leave no fingerprints, he wrapped a handkerchief around his fingers. He made his way into Loretta's parlor. He opened the top drawer where she'd shown Willie the photo of Elena at her baptism. Not much else in there, a checkbook with no register plus three bills to "Antonio Cornero" had been sent to this address. Loretta'd written checks for each of them to Santa Ana Water, Edison Power, and Pacific Tel and Tel. "Payment in full."

They must have some type of arrangement. Willie checked the drawer below and found four Marlboro cartons plus a dozen books of matches. They were from ships, the *S.S. Rex*; a pair were from the *S.S. Tango*. Two from The Meadows Club on Boulder Highway just outside Las Vegas.

All of the remaining drawers were empty.

He pressed the drawers shut. His interest had been piqued. He kept exploring. All the kitchen drawers were full, but he found nothing there of interest. Dusty utensils. Willie imagined they'd been there when she'd moved in. Nothing but kitsch up on her shelves looked like Loretta had disturbed it. The salt and pepper shakers smelled like they'd been sanitized with Windex. Her Wheaties Anchor-Hocking glassware appeared spotless.

He made his way back to the bedrooms. He found nothing in the closets. The only clothes were in his guest room still packed up in Stanley's suitcase. The place felt like a hotel plopped in a residential neighborhood. The last door, to Loretta's room, was locked.

He made his way back to his bedroom. *What was the deal with Loretta?* He found the picture of Elena that had dried out in his wallet. She looked so innocent, so young when he compared her to Loretta. Smoking aged Loretta, wrinkled the edges of her lips and deepened worry lines that creased above her eyebrows. Such a pity.

Willie sat next to his Charley Boards. Tomorrow he'd find out if he could sell them. Yes, his Spanish was pathetic, but the shopkeepers spoke English. It was his day job, besides looking for Elena. He would need to double down and find a way to do them both.

Willie thought about Elena.

He recalled her tender kiss, her gentle laugh, the way her face looked when she shook out her dark hair and met his gaze while they held hands. She didn't say much, but her eyes could write a book saying she loved him. "*Te adoro, Willie.*" Her scent carried that hint of sage and roses as she told him his soft touch could leave her feeling like a butterfly.

She loved butterflies. Loved to watch them. Elena knew them all by name: monarchs, swallowtails, painted ladies, mourning cloaks, and sulfurs. She would smile at lazy swallowtails gliding through the sycamores, then pirouetting up from underneath live oaks, dancing in spirals.

Willie felt butterflies himself, but these were fluttering in his stomach. He touched her fingers. She clenched his hand as if she dared not let him go.

She'd laughed. "*Podemos volar como mariposas juntos.*" She had pointed. There were monarchs in the milkweed by the Santa Ana River. A pair of them ascended toward the sun. "They are like us," she'd said. "Most happy when together."

Feeling warm, he made his way outside to bathtub Virgin Mary, where Willie prayed for a *milagro*. Maybe, that's why Mary was there. Standing upright in her tub she smiled almost like Elena. Yeah, it seemed weird enough.

But on some nights, even miracles seemed possible.

CHAPTER VII

MONDAY, MARCH 14

It had been weeks since the last time Willie had dreamed about Elena. Her fleeting image began fading when he fought to hold it close, the dress she'd worn to Irvine Park, the searing sparkle in her empathetic eyes, so glad to see him, like she loved him, had believed in him when no one in his life save for Elena gave a damn.

But she was fading. He remembered she had whispered "Adios," which meant, "To God" like she was leaving for a journey far away. Elena told him not to cry. Told him "Te amo. Te adoro," and the soft scent of her breath somehow was filling up the forest full of sycamores and toyons as her image drifted off toward the moon leaving an emptiness he knew that he could never fill again.

Elena waved, flashing a smile like the Bathtub Virgin Mary, before she fragmented and vanished behind a cloud of mariposas.

Monarch butterflies had always been her favorite.

Willie woke up with the roosters to a picture-postcard morning, He grabbed his Charlie Boards and hid them in a plain brown paper bag in case some cops frowned on his enterprise. He didn't know the ropes yet. But two sales were all he needed to come home with forty dollars.

It was so early that the barbershop pole hadn't been turned on yet. Helms Bakery and Adohr Farms trucks cast extended morning shadows. Willie watched. Inside the barbershop, José maneuvered a battered wooden push-broom around green cast-iron barber chairs and cabinets. José straightened up his comic books and girlie magazines on his front table for his customers to look at.

When Willie stepped inside the shop, the cowbell jongled on the entrance door. He was greeted with the usual scents of Barbasol and hair oil. Willie wondered why he hadn't asked José about Elena. He would ask him in a minute. Right now, he had to make a sale, and José could make a ton of extra money off these Charley Boards.

It almost seemed a natural alliance.

Willie shut the door behind him. He looked over his shoulder. Morning sun poured though the glass, showcasing beard stubble and clips of male hair on gray linoleum.

José looked up, and he frowned. "We not open yet. *Lo siento.*"

Willie glanced down at his wristwatch. Ten to eight. He inhaled. "*No problema,*" Willie answered in the deepest voice he could. "But this is business. *Negocios.*" He put a finger to his lips. "I think you'll like this one," said Willie. "I found a simple deal to help you make more money." He looked into José's eyes.

Willie smiled.

Wide.

It shocked Willie to hear himself sound so much like a huckster.

"And what might that be?" asked José.

Willie took a deeper breath. He reached into his sack.

"Ever seen one of these babies?" Willie asked. Handing José one of the Charley Boards, he smiled even wider. He waited for the customer to speak.

"*¿Y que es ese?*"

"*Es un* Charley Board." Willie studied José's face.

The barber held it in his hands like they were clutched around a steering wheel.

Willie told him how the board could earn him money."

"Is legal, Willie?"

"No one knows. But no one's passed a law against them," Willie said. "Yet."

José looked outside his barbershop and made a funny face. He shut the blinds.

"How many Charley Boards you have?"

"Just two right now."

"Can I get more?"

"How many barbershops you own?" Willie said, laughing.

"For my family, six uncles and six cousins." José shrugged. He handed Willie forty dollars from the register.

"So twelve?"

Willie realized he'd scored the first big sale of his life as José nodded. "Just don't go selling any squares to the police, or they'll get jealous." Willie said. An understanding warmed the barbershop as José flipped the switch on by the front window.

The barber pole lit up and started turning.

Willie placed the cash into his wallet. He'd forgotten about Elena. He closed his eyes and said a prayer. One more question.

This one's personal. He showed Willie the photograph. "You know her? Name's Elena."

José stared outside across the street.

"She remind me of someone else. Um, Valenzuela." José said. "She called Loretta Valenzuela. Very flirty."

"Come here often?"

"Once a month. Comes here with sailor man from Long Beach. Tattooed forearm. Jack of diamonds with a knife stuck through one eyeball gushing blood. Is all I know about the sailor."

"*Muchas gracias, José*."

"*De nada*. Bring me more Charley Boards, okay?"

"Will do," said Willie. He looked outside through the front window. He'd made a sale. He was certain that would make Enrico happy.

But Willie hadn't heard a word on what had happened to Elena. For all his efforts, people acted like the girl had never existed. Of course she had, he told himself. He'd seen the photo of her baptism, recalled her kiss, their times together. She had been his *mariposa*, his lovely butterfly, a monarch who reflected the orange sunrise. It's not as if he'd made things up. Her smile was seared into his memories so deep he felt he'd die if he gave up on trying to find her. But he was running out of leads. Elena's trail had gone cold. He shook his head feeling a part of him inside begin to die.

Willie feared that it was only the beginning.

"So, what's the word, hummingbird?" Loretta waved to Willie from the doorstep of her bungalow. He made his way up Olive

Street. His mind whirled with euphoria. He'd just made forty bucks in sales at José's, but there was something in Loretta's voice that jarred him.

He'd caught a slight edge in her voice, as if she'd figured out he'd snooped around her house. He'd been careful. And it's not like he had found anything special, save for the absence of much evidence Loretta even lived there. But something in her tone gave Willie pause.

She wore a muted floral sundress with a pair of jaded sunglasses. It wasn't the Loretta that the world was used to seeing. This morning she talked slower than her normal rapid English.

"Sold my Charlie Boards." Willie grinned.

Loretta didn't smile back. A radio played *mariachi* music down the hall.

She looked at Willie, motioned, and then whispered, "Come inside."

Shadows spilling through the picture window flowed across the carpet in the parlor as he followed her into her tiny kitchen. Loretta poured herself some coffee. Took a sip and set it down. Sat at her table. Placed her forehead in her palms and calmly stared down at her tablecloth while Willie wondered what was going on.

Then she stood up. Walked to her bedroom. She returned, bringing an envelope of photographs in black and white. The pier reminded him of Seal Beach. There was a body in the sand, curled up and covered up with seaweed like a piece of human driftwood on the beach had somehow washed onto the shore during the night.

"You know her, Willie?" Loretta's voice cracked.

Willie didn't answer. His voice seemed to be frozen in a different place and time. Like he'd been ambushed. He took a hard look at the photograph. A chill fully immersed him, and time froze as Willie's heart stopped in mid-beat.

He saw the face. Glanced at Loretta.

Willie whispered back, "Elena?"

She met his gaze. It *was* Elena. It was written in her eyes.

He had meant it as a question, but it wasn't. It had come out as a certainty. Pale lips Willie had kissed, covered with crabs and flies, and seaweed. Dark matted hair, no longer radiant, a face frozen in terror on a torso like a wax-museum mannequin.

Stark naked.

Willie fought to breathe.

There was no way he could cover up his horror as the pain rose up inside him. Acid crawled up Willie's throat. He gulped it down. He felt a chill. Glanced at Loretta. "Where'd you get these?"

"I have friends."

"What sort of friends? They haven't even marked the crime scene yet, Loretta."

There were no cops in the photo. Just a body on a beach framed by the white strip of the photograph edge, scalloped on all sides.

"My friend works for *The Santa Ana Register*."

"But how did *you* get this?"

"He gave them to me."

"Why?"

The room felt colder than an ice house.

A tear welled in her eye. "Why don't you ever trust me, Willie?" Her eyes pleaded for mercy.

He put his hand over his mouth. He'd had no reason to attack her. He met her gaze and saw her weeping. Perhaps there wasn't any crime, and poor Elena had been washed away by floods out to the ocean, and the sea had tossed her back, a naked corpse covered with kelp, and there was nobody to blame except the rains.

Outside, a noisy truck on Olive seemed in dire need of a muffler. Then it passed.

The kitchen felt quiet as a morgue, save for the faint hum of the wall clock and the drone of an announcer speaking Spanish from the Sears Silvertone radio in her bedroom down the hall.

Loretta wiped a tear.

And then her chest began to undulate. She moaned the name "Elena," several times.

Willie's heart began to jackhammer.

Loretta stood. She made her way toward the sink. She grabbed a dish towel. Smeared her tears and half the makeup from her face.

He rose to help her.

She collapsed into his arms, shaking and writhing, and her hair covered her face, and Willie noticed she smelled so much like Elena. But they were sisters. She dug her chin into his shoulder, and her arms circled his back to press him tight against her womanhood so Willie wasn't quite sure what to think.

Until his tears came.

Willie held her in the kitchen. Loretta's heartbeat throbbed against the muscles in his chest in longing agony. Her arms against his back pulled him up close. He felt her breath; it felt exactly like Elena's; the soft flesh of her back began to feel the way things had at Irvine Park, the day Elena had invited him to join her at a picnic. They had found themselves alone beneath the California oaks, and there was aching. There was longing. Willie's head bowed down. He breathed. And then he lifted up his head and felt the sunshine on his back, but it was coming through Loretta's kitchen window.

Loretta looked at him. Her lips touched his.

Willie tried to pause.

But it was feeling like a dream, and he surrendered to the moment. Loretta made him feel strong the way Elena had, and suddenly he longed to hold her tighter. Felt their lips molding together, and his tears fused in with hers, and they were walking toward the bedroom, and Loretta closed the door.

She turned the light out.

Pulled the curtains.

A *marimba* song was playing on her radio. From Mexico. Loretta said the name was *Frenesí,* Spanish for frenzy. The lyrics *Bésame con frenesí* resounded off her ceiling, and their bodies found the rhythm, and they melded into one.

He felt warm beneath the covers with her body close against his. They pulsated together and Loretta's hot breath filled up Willie's throat.

And for the first time in his life Willie was in a woman's bedroom where she showed him what Elena never had.

CHAPTER VIII

TUESDAY, MARCH 22

More than a week had passed since Willie'd learned the sad news of Elena. His girlfriend's death consumed his thoughts, even though business had been good. He'd borrowed money from the Crocker Bank and bought a box of twelve more Charlie Boards he carried in a plain brown paper grocery sack from Shopping Bag. Today he planned to sell them to José.

The cowbell on the door clattered as Willie stepped inside of José's barbershop. No customers so far. He'd timed it well. José was sitting on his stool reading a girlie magazine next to his brass NCR register, its keys gummed up with Wildroot. *"Ito ay malungkot."* A pause. José's white smock covered his cowboy shirt. He glanced up with a serious expression as he chatted on the telephone. Willie didn't know the dialect. Only a few words sounded anything like Spanish.

"Paalam." José said sadly. He shook his head, setting the handset in its cradle like he worried it might shatter in his grip. Turning, José glanced at the floor. He was still shaking

his head. He wiped his forehead and looked up. "G'mornin', Willie." José sighed.

"Wh-who was that?"

"My second cousin is a nurse down at the coroner's. They find this girl at Seal Beach."

Willie was jarred to full alert. He held his breath.

"They find man's semen in her. Means the girl gets raped after the floods. Then someone tries to make it look as though she drowns."

"You just said what?"

José repeated it. Each word felt like a knife through Willie's gut. His thoughts spun so hard he felt dizzy, stumbled sideways, bumped his hip against drab-olive painted wainscotting. He forced himself to breathe and finally straightened. "That's what I thought you said," voiced Willie in a stammer.

He looked up.

The shop felt colder than a butcher shop as Willie stared outside. KIEV was playing Bob Wills singing, "I'm a Ding Dong Daddy." Willie tried to keep his breakfast down. His stomach felt like glass. A fan spun overhead, moaning aloud as if it understood his agony. It had to be Elena at the coroner's.

They'd raped her.

And newspapers would never print the story.

Because *The Santa Ana Register* was only about white people. Her people's newspaper, *La Opinión,* was clear up in L.A. They seldom came down to Orange County. It was somewhere on the fringes where it seemed nobody cared if someone hurt you.

Or raped you.

Or killed the only girl you'd ever loved.

He fought back rage, because this was not what Willie'd come to talk about.

He braced himself. He swallowed pain and steeled his wilting will. Persperation on his forehead dripped like cold sweat off a beer can. Willie tried to shake it off. "I brought those Charlie Boards you wanted," Willie said. He looked away. Time to focus on his business.

A Model A turned left on Third Street.

Gene Autry's voice replaced Bob Wills. *Tumbling Tumbleweeds* were echoing off walls.

"How many boards?"

Willie said, "Twelve."

"What? Do you think I'm made of money?"

"You asked for twelve."

José kept staring at the floor. "Allright, allright," he said. "But that's enough for now. I'll take them all. But no more Charlie Boards. I need to earn my money back. And then I come and talk to you, okay?" He made his way toward the register as Willie gave the twelve boards to José.

The telephone rang. José let it ring.

Willie had to wipe his palm before he shook José's big hand, then looked away.

José asked, "You okay, there, Willie?"

Willie stood mum.

José opened the cash drawer on the register. The bell chimed through the barbershop. He counted Willie's money out in twenties.

Willie counted it again. He stuffed the bills into his trousers. Never before had he held onto so much money.

But he could not enjoy it now. His heart was sick about Elena.

Willie turned and slowly asked, "José, what language were you speaking?"

"We speak Tagalog." José blushed. "He is my cousin."

"You aren't – Mexican?"

"Only half. Other half is Filipino from Luzon. Home of my mother near Manila." José smiled.

"But you look...."

"Mexican? Half the people in Manila are part Mexican," José said. "The Spanish sailors need more crewpeople to fully man their galleons to the Orient. So they grab *Indios* from Mexico and leave us in Manila. No point in bringing us to Spain if we are brown." He gave a shrug.

But right now, Willie didn't care about the Philippines. He made a fist. Stretched out his hand. "What did you learn about the girl?" His teeth were gritted, but Jose was just the messenger.

"At Seal Beach?"

"What do you know? She was...." He pounded on a barber chair. "*...m-mi novia.*" His voice broke.

José's head tilted. "You need somebody to talk to?"

"She was RAPED."

"I know. I know, and there is nothing we can do."

"Most likely murdered." Willie felt his heart machine-gun. He was on the edge of tears and bit back rage as the reality sank in. Nobody cared. No point in calling in the types who would ignore him.

"Of course. We'll just call the police." Willie felt acid in his voice laced in with sarcasm. He laughed. "Mister policeman is our friend. Learned it in grammar school." He glanced toward the mirror and cracked his knuckles.

"The police don't give a damn about us," José made a face. "Last time some thief holds up my store this copper shows up with his partner. He pulls his eyes back and makes fun of me. He tells me 'Rotsa ruck,' and then his partner laughs out loud as if a robbery is not so big a deal. Policeman doesn't even file a report. He just makes jokes." José grimaced as he slammed the cash drawer shut so hard it rattled all the tonic bottles perched behind the barber chairs.

And then he shook his head. "Willie, there ain't much we can do here. We aren't welcome. People only choose to see us when they need something." He glanced at Willie, and he frowned. "Most of them see us as a nuisance. Sad but true. And then they turn on us the day we need a favor."

Willie shut the door so softly that the cowbell didn't jangle.

Then he made his way up Third Street. There were clouds, and it was sweltering, but strangely Willie felt a chill cold as the City he'd grown up in. Cold as – Mildred. He set his jaw and watched the traffic as the GO signal let traffic flow on Main Street.

A DON'T WALK light changed to WALK.

He crossed the street watching a group of shoppers climb aboard a Red Car. If the police refused to do their jobs, he'd need to do it for them. He remembered Mr. Norton at the farmhouse out by Atwood.

The man had lied.

Willie thought he might know why.

A sideways grin.

Tomorrow he'd make sure he paid that man a little visit.

He balled his fists and made his way along a crumbling concrete sidewalk on his way toward Josefina's where he had another job.

Tomorrow he would take a ride to Atwood.

#

CHAPTER IX

ORANGE: TUESDAY, MARCH 22

Riding the Red Car north from Santa Ana, Willie cracked his knuckles. He felt nervous and thumped a fist against his palm a dozen times. He suspected that the Nortons were evasive for a reason but didn't know whether they'd raped Elena, murdered her, or both. He leaned back, making a plan to ambush Norton and learn the truth. Willie swallowed. There were truths he feared he might not care to learn. But Elena deserved someone in her corner.

He knew the Nortons owned a shotgun, but Willie wasn't in a hurry. He could wait for the old lady to leave home to drive to Fullerton. Then he'd jump Norton in his orchards. Willie feared that might be tricky. There were neighbors, so he had to keep things quiet if he could. Plus, he wouldn't know if Norton had a knife.

First, he'd need to find the barn, the one they swore never existed. Willie'd been there. He knew it had been set on concrete footings. Foundations didn't disappear the way the barn had washed away. He'd find the footings. Spend an hour and a half. Do some reconnaissance and wait for Mrs. Norton to take off.

The northbound Red Car paused at Orange and then continued up toward Marlboro, a platform between Taft and Vista Avenues north of town. That was where the trolley ended. Willie tugged the cable, wondering why he'd bothered signaling when only the conductor and himself were still remaining on the trolley.

The conductor glared at Willie. He lit himself an L&M and stared outside at lemon orchards through the window. He exhaled. The trolley groaned. It slowed, and sparks flew from the pantograph above. Willie figured he would need to walk five miles to see Norton.

Just north of Marlboro, a wye onto the Southern Pacific tracks permitted the trolley to turn around after a freight train had gone by. Willie exited the muddy steel steps next to the platform. As he walked north on Santa Fe tracks toward the Santa Ana River, he recalled his last trip up here. Then, he'd been more optimistic. Back then, he'd thought Pop was his father. He'd thought the cops looked out for everyone. He hadn't known he was part-Mexican, had known nothing about gambling in Orange County. He'd been a virgin and Elena'd been one too. Plus, now he missed the carefree days when he'd had a virgin mind.

Everything in Willie's life had changed.

Now even Mexicans looked down on him, except for Josefina and Loretta. Nobody trusted him. He seemed to be in limbo, too dark-skinned to pass for white and too light-skinned to be a Mexican. People weren't sure who he was or who his friends were anymore. They called him *güero.* God, it felt lonely. People weren't like his Elena who'd adored him. Or *Abuelo*. Willie missed them both so much.

He took the same route as before, walking up Orange-Olive Road. The railroad bridge was still washed out. He walked a mile east to Jefferson. There, an old concrete low-water crossing forded the Santa Ana River.

The water depth now barely cleared his ankles.

He took his shoes off and his socks, then rolled his jeans above his knees. It was a beautiful spring day, and Willie wished he could enjoy it. But he had matters to attend to. Important business for Elena. He splashed across, holding shoes and socks aloft in his right hand, smelling the scents of sage and mugwort that were wafting down the canyon.

On the north side of the river, Willie ducked into an orchard. He put his shoes and socks back on again and doubled down to business.

Sprays of mustard flowers fanned between the aisles of Valencias running north beside the roadway. Willie found an irrigation ditch. He followed it. The landmarks seemed, at last, to look familiar: the giant oak he once had climbed up with Elena rose above him. There they'd spent an afternoon up in the branches watching swallowtails dancing in the breezes off the Santa Ana Mountains. That was where Elena had first kissed him.

"Te adoro, Willie." He couldn't flush those words out of his mind. It wasn't everyday a woman said she loved him.

He had never met a woman who could kiss quite like Elena. Make him feel strong, as if he mattered, her kisses warming him like freshly baked *tamales* she wrapped in tinfoil after mass at Irvine Park where they would meet before the floods destroyed their lives.

At the clearing where the barn had been, he glanced over his shoulders. Coast was clear. He made his way beyond a water pump and found the concrete rectangle, the footing where the barn structure had stood. He had his proof. Norton had lied about the barn.

What other lies had Norton told him?

Willie lay in wait. He'd soon find out. The palpitations of his heart kept him alert.

If he sat still, his chance would come. An auto engine started up. It was the Cadillac. The car rolled down the driveway in reverse. It backed onto Richfield Road with Mrs. Norton at the wheel. She held her grocery list in-hand. Looked like she planned to do some shopping.

He watched the woman drive away. This might take a couple of hours. He checked his watch. Three thirty-five, at least two hours before sundown.

Right on schedule, Mr. Norton made his way out of his house, wearing a pair of gray suspenders over a red shirt and blue Levis. Willie crouched down on his knees behind an oleander bush.

He waited. Not a sound.

Norton came whistling his direction. Walked right past him.

Leaping up, Willie grabbed Norton in a headlock.

"Hey? Who are...?"

A moment's struggle. Willie tightened up his grip around the throat.

Norton was whimpering and pleading.

"Shut up old man, or I choke harder."

"What you want?"

"We need to talk about the barn."

"There is no barn." Norton glared at him. His build and height were similar to Willie's but he was older, forty-something, giving Willie an advantage.

"Liar," said Willie. He muscled Norton toward the remnants of the barn and asked again. "How about *this* barn?" He shoved Norton to the dirt.

Norton rose, looking dumbfounded. "You worthless piece of greaser shit." He threw a punch.

Willie ducked.

A second landed on his jaw. He rubbed his mouth and stepped away. Spit some blood onto the dirt.

Willie thought about Elena. He knew Norton could fight dirty.

So would Willie. He charged the man.

Norton grabbed a two-by-six. Swung it toward Willie like a baseball bat. He missed and fell off-balance.

Willie charged him, punched a left jab into Norton, who stepped back. He followed up with a right hook to Norton's ear that made him stagger. A hard-left cross into the chest. An uppercut to Norton's jaw. He crumpled over. Willie hammered Norton's gut. Then threw a smash across the jaw.

Norton cussed and spit a tooth at Willie's face.

Rage arose in Willie. Another uppercut. A hard right to the temple.

Norton staggered and fell back, banging his head against a rock.

He was knocked out.

Crap! thought Willie as he panicked. He'd need to shake him back to consciousness to question him. He slapped him. Several times.

Norton moaned and clutched a rib like it was broken.

"All right, mister," Willie said. "Let's hear the truth." He glared at Norton.

Blood seeped from a gash above his eye. The lips were swollen.

"You better sing like a canary, or I'll knock out *all* your teeth." He found a rag in Norton's yard and wiped warm blood from off his lips. Left eye was swollen, but the other eye was staring straight at Willie.

"Okay, I saw her."

"You saw Elena. Did you touch her? Did you…?"

"No."

He spat the word, glaring at Willie. He was struggling just to breathe.

Willie offered him some water, not too sure if he believed him.

Norton took a sip. He caught his breath. Began to gasp. He was evidently dizzy. "She was living in this barn, you fool. Loretta paid me off."

"How much?" asked Willie, leaning back, glad to finally get a couple answers that checked out.

"Eighty a month to rent the place out to her father."

"Her *Abuelo*?"

"Loretta's *father*."

"I thought Elena had a sister."

"She has two. But they're in Mexico. Deported. Hauled away in big green trucks by the police."

"I thought Loretta was...."

"Their mother," Norton hissed. "What did you think?"

It was Willie's turn to gasp.

He looked around. It seemed Loretta hadn't told him the whole truth, had led him on. Willie stepped back, and his head spun. It made sense she had that photo after all. Her whole story had smelled fishier than a Newport Harbor bait tank.

A motorcar, a red LaSalle sputtered north on Richfield Road. Thank God it wasn't Mrs. Norton. The car drove straight past Norton's house and kept on going.

Willie glanced down at his watch and fought back panic. She could come back any minute. He'd just beaten up her husband. But he'd just learned who Loretta really was. He couldn't stop yet.

"Where does Loretta make her money?" It was a pure shot in the dark.

But Norton answered. "She's a hostess on the *Tango* and the *Rex*."

"The *S.S. Tango?*" He recalled seing those matchbooks in her dresser. Dots connected.

"The gambling boats." Norton struggled for a breath. "I assume she provides favors to high rollers."

"What sort of favors?" His temples throbbed.

"Jeez, do I have to draw a picture? Are you stupid? It's how she paid me off to take care of Elena and *Abuelo*."

Willie felt his heart implode inside him.

He'd been so stinking naïve. They had seemed like decent people, working hard to make a living. That was probably the truth. But they were living in the shadows, a world he knew little about, where people did the things they had to to survive, the way Loretta did to take care of her family. Those who didn't.... He glanced at Norton, who had just provided missing information. ... He had seen some being loaded onto trucks. Shipped off to Mexico, deported. Things were starting to make sense.

"Where's *Abuelo?*" Willie asked.

"Elena said she saw him drown."

"You *saw* Elena?" His heart raced. He was finally nearing paydirt.

"She begged for help during the storm. Only my wife, she don't like wetbacks. It's nothing personal. I gave Elena a few bucks and told her, 'Scram.' Dropped a nickel. Phoned Loretta. Told the truth, I couldn't help her. What was I supposed to do now that I didn't have a barn?"

"You have a house," Willie fired back.

Norton stared at him. "You crazy? You really think my wife would share a house with greasers?"

Willie spat in Norton's eye. He heard a car engine. Mrs. Norton. She was returning in her Cadillac. She swerved into the driveway, crunching gravel.

Furious, Willie threw a punch, knocking Norton back to sleep. He was still breathing. Had a pulse. The cut above the eye was clotted. Willie couldn't stick around. The cops would be here soon enough, and Willie didn't want the old lady to see him.

He made a dash into the orchard. He staggered west along Placentia-Yorba Boulevard. In Placentia he found a tavern with a pay phone right outside. There Willie called the cops and told them about Norton. Thank God no one knew who Willie was. Good thing he'd never told them. The most they'd know was they had seen him a few times around Elena.

"He's beat up bad," Willie gasped out." He had one eye swollen shut. Behind the barn by Richfield Road."

"Sir, what's your name?"

Willie hung up. He used the tail of his shirt to wipe his prints from off the handset. Willie stepped outside and elbowed the phone booth's glass door shut behind him.

Norton's blood was spattered all over his hands and up his sleeves. Willie panicked. He had to wash away the evidence, and soon. He made his way down to the Santa Ana River. Waded in. Here it was deeper, and the river's ripples shimmered in the night beneath a full moon that reflected off the water.

Dried blood swirled into the waters, and the evidence was gone. Willie hoped there wouldn't be any infection.

He waded out.

He shook the river from his clothes and shivered southward toward Orange. His eyelids felt like weights. He saw the lights beyond the groves.

Then it dawned on him he didn't have a clue who'd raped Elena, or how she'd died, or even if she had been murdered.

It was so dark it took an hour and a half to walk to Orange. Nothing was open when he got there. He took a nap behind a building. Someone had *raped* Elena. Willie still had no clue who that was. But he knew one thing. If Elena'd needed help, where would she go? To find her mother who had always taken care of her and grandpa. So where, then, would Loretta be? Willie had a hunch it was the gambling ships. Those matchbooks in Loretta's chest of drawers contained the phone numbers. He'd call them. Say he was looking for Loretta Valenzuela. With any luck he'd find out which ship she was on.

And track her down.

Except right now Willie felt too tired to keep going.

CHAPTER X

SANTA ANA: THURSDAY, MARCH 24

From Page 2 of *The Santa Ana Register*

PLACENTIA ORCHARDMAN ASSAULTED OUTSIDE BARN IN RICHFIELD GROVES

After receiving a phantom tip, Orange County sheriffs rushed to an orange grove near Placentia where a local orchardman had been assaulted. Police say 44-year-old Lawrence Richard Norton, who owns the orchard, had been brutally attacked by vagrant Mexicans and left outside his barn to be found bleeding and unconscious.

Norton, whose injuries include broken ribs, a concussion, and cuts and bruises is recuperating at Orange County General. Norton's wife, Priscilla Norton, when interviewed by local sheriffs, claims the incident occurred during her shopping trip to Fullerton. She reported several Mexicans were spotted near her property, and looters had been active after the Santa Ana River floods. Norton's wallet was intact. Police are still investigating. Sheriffs advise all local residents to stay inside their homes and take no chances should any Mexicans be seen lurking in their neighborhoods.

The stench of cigarettes inside Loretta's kitchen was so strong a man could build himself a house on it and add a second story. Willie had stopped by for some coffee and to change into fresh clothes. Loretta wasn't home when he got in.

There were no notes. Her bedroom door was locked. He hadn't seen her for two days, since before he'd taken off to get to Atwood on the Red Car. Willie peeked inside the dresser drawer. He scribbled down some numbers for the *S.S. Rex, the S.S. Tango,* and The Meadows in Las Vegas.

That narrowed matters down a bit, but maybe not enough to find Loretta. He scanned the newspaper. The headline on page 2 gave him a start. He read the article. Police had turned up Norton. He was happy Norton's wife, with her contempt for all things Mexican, had inadvertently provided all those false leads to *The Register*.

Still Willie needed to lay low. And with that gash across his brow, people could see he had been fighting and put two plus two together. He'd need to stick to his own kind. Stay away from any *güeros*. Take a trip out on a water taxi, find out where the *Rex* was or the *Tango,* maybe find out how Loretta made her living.

He made a phone call.

The person at the *S.S. Tango* number introduced herself as Alice.

"I'd like to book a room," said Willie. "On the *Tango*. I'll be leaving from Orange County."

"Have you stayed here?"

"No," Willie replied. "I pulled your number off a matchbook cover. Got it from a friend. Her name's Loretta Valenzuela."

"Oh," the phone voice said. She seemed to recognize the name. A good sign.

I'll need a water taxi ride out to the ship from Newport Beach."

"We leave from Seal Beach or Long Beach."

"Nothing from Newport?"

"Not that we advertise."

"But you *have* something," said Willie.

"For two bucks more. Boat leaves Monday, the 28th."

"*No problema,*" Willie said, feeling a smile cross his face.

"Suit yourself," said Alice.

Willie fished a pen out of his trousers and scrawled directions to the Balboa Pavilion on a scratchpad.

"Water Taxi Number 8 leaves the dock at six a.m. for Catalina."

"But I'm not going to Catalina," Willie said.

Alice laughed. "In thirty minutes, you'll be dropped off at the *Tango*. It's a ruse."

"Don't the police know what you're doing?"

"Cops don't care. Everything's legal. Ships are five miles offshore, out where the law doesn't apply."

"I meant the water taxi part."

"Helps customers keep up appearances. Family drops 'em off in Newport for a fishing trip to Avalon. We can't tell ladies their husbands are off gambling. Bad for business."

It made sense. That was why the Newport boats weren't advertised. "I'll take one ticket," Willie said, "And a return trip the next day."

"That will be ten dollars in cash."

Willie had the money.

But it felt shady. Why was everyone in Orange County lying about water taxis, barns, and other things that didn't matter? Why had they lied about Elena? Why had they lied about his father? Why had Loretta said Elena was her sister, not her daughter? It bothered Willie. Sometimes even made him sick the more he thought about it. Why was everybody lying about something?

Willie refolded the newspaper, and replaced it on the coffee table, showing the front page. He'd need to cover up his tracks. Too much was happening. Norton might tip off the cops once he got healthy, and they would certainly come looking for Willie. Time was running out.

Willie staggered to his bedroom to catch a half an hour's sleep. In forty minutes, he would need to be at work for Josefina. As his head sank into pillows, Willie had a funny thought. Everyone he knew about was facing the same fate. They were irrelevant, and no one gave a crap that they existed. Life was like this huge roulette table the size of Orange County. You kept laying down your money. But the odds were stacked against you. Anyone who did the math knew how the house would always win. People in China called it "Death by a Thousand Cuts."

But no one talked about it. Everyone kept plopping down their money in despair, till they went broke, and then they died with no one left to pay the bills.

Maybe that's why everyone was lying, Willie thought.

He held his breath when it occurred to him that he was lying too.

He couldn't think about that now. He had a job in fifteen minutes.

He put his shoes on and he hurried off to work at Josefina's. He noticed now his heart was pounding hard.

SATURDAY, MARCH 26

Three days had passed since Willie's visit up to Atwood and the fight. No more news about the Nortons in *The Santa Ana Register.* No news was good news, Willie figured. He was pretty sure he hadn't left a trail, but from now on he could not return to Atwood.

Rays of sunset stabbed like daggers through the glass at Josefina's, bleeding red across the dusty concrete floor between the shadows. It made the floor look like a monolithic brick covered with sawdust. Willie saw Enrico in the corner at his table.

Willie'd brought two-hundred dollars. Enough for twenty Charlie Boards. He walked toward Enrico with the money in his fist. Asked, "Where's Loretta?"

Enrico stared across the street toward his Auburn. "She isn't stopping by this evening. Sorry, Loretta's out of town."

"So, where'd she go?"

Enrico shrugged. "Am I Loretta's keeper? And you don't *want* to know, *hermano*. I'm only here to sell you Charlie Boards, *capisce*? They're getting scarce. Suicide Jack says there's a shortage."

"Suicide Jack?"

"My supplier. Kid, I don't get these from the Tooth Fairy."

"How many Charlie Boards?"

"Two dozen."

"I only got two-hundred dollars."

"Take the other four on credit."

Willie froze. He didn't want them. He got nervous owing money, but he needed information on Loretta. He bit his tongue. Fought back nerves. "Fine, I'll take them."

He payed Enrico, leaving two twenties in his pocket for the water taxi, food out on the *Tango*, and his room.

Enrico shoved the bills into his pockets and leaned back, puffing his Camel cigarette.

Willie cleared his throat. "I need to know about Loretta, though."

"What did I just tell you?"

Willie looked up. He slammed his fist down on the table. His throat tightened. "Where's Loretta? And who the hell's Tony Cornero?" Willie whispered. "And why's Loretta have a matchbook from the *Tango* and the *Rex*?"

Enrico puffed his cigarette and smiled wide. The room felt musty. Rico shrugged. "Maybe Loretta likes to gamble."

"Bullfrog, Rico. You know better. Even I know there's more to it." Willie's pulse hammered his temples.

"Follow your hunch, then," Rico deadpanned. He glanced down.

"Are you sayin'...?" Willie's mind flashed to the things he'd learned from Norton. She was a hostess on a gambling ship, but clearly there was more.

Rico snuffed his cigarette out. "I didn't tell you a damn thing. I only asked you to sell Charlie Boards. You still owe me forty bucks. I'll be expecting all my money in the mail by next week."

He gave Willie the address, a P.O. box up in Long Beach.

Rico grabbed his hat and stood, making a beeline toward the door.

The edgy tone in Rico's voice said Willie'd stepped on a few nerves. And something else told him he'd need to find another line of work. The Charlie Board gig seemed too easy. There was some angle to it Willie didn't know about, but any day the other shoe would drop.

It made him nervous. It also troubled him he'd beat up old man Norton.

But right now, Willie had to go offshore and find Loretta.

CHAPTER XI

NEWPORT BEACH: MONDAY, MARCH 28

Layered clouds off Newport Harbor seemed to bleed on the horizon. Willie hadn't found his sea legs, and the water taxi gave him indigestion. He clutched his seat cushion. It didn't seem to help. The ocean reeked of kelp and fish, and battered dories were returning from their night runs, bringing tuna stacked four-high across their decks. A flock of gulls circled the fishing boats and screeched like angry children. Willie steeled himself, determined to learn who had raped Elena.

Salt spray peppered Willie's face and stung his weary eyes. Water Taxi Number 8 had navigated out the breakwater, pointed toward Catalina's distant silhouette. Beneath the tattered dark green awning, Willie stared into the headwinds. In half an hour he would board the *Tango,* four miles offshore. After that, all bets were off. He hoped to run into Loretta. They'd seemed to recognize her name when he had used it on the phone. If not, he'd try the S.S. Rex if the cops didn't find out he'd beat up Norton and come calling with their badges.

The water taxi turned, making a hard right to the starboard. Willie watched a pelican that circled overhead. He worried what Loretta'd think if he surprised her at her workplace, but she'd lied to him. She'd told him that Elena was her sister. She was her *daughter*. Willie wondered what other lies Loretta'd told him.

From the mainland, starry lights flickered from Signal Hill and Long Beach. He checked his wristwatch. Quarter-to-seven. A blip appeared on the horizon. It turned out to be a tanker ship that sailed in toward Long Beach. Tugboats pulled it in toward the harbor.

Willie panicked. He'd forgotten to call in to Josefina and tell her he couldn't work tonight. That would not go over well, especially lately. The kitchen help had somehow turned against him. He understood they didn't trust him. His absence only made things worse, and if the Charley Boards went south, he wasn't sure what he'd do next.

Someone hollered from the bow, "*S.S. Tango* to our port."

The gambling ship looked like a barge with a casino built atop it. Strings of lights hung from a masthead toward the gunwales and the bow. A row of cabins toward the rear was still lit up to greet the sunrise. Big black letters on the port side of the ship read "S.S. TANGO."

The gambling ship grew larger. Its foghorn blared out through the mist. The water taxi answered in what seemed to be a code. A stranger rose up from his seat across the water taxi deck. He frowned. His dirty shirtsleeves were rolled up above his elbows. He lit a Camel. His forearm muscles were as big as Willie's calves and bore a tattoo of a playing card that wrapped around his wrists.

That jack of diamonds looked disturbed. He'd plunged a knife into his eye socket, and blood was squirting out of it. The jack's mouth spread in horror in the same shape as a scream. The stranger looked like someone Willie didn't care to meet.

The playing card made Willie shudder. Some tattoos were meant to do that. A jagged scar on the man's cheek showed pea-size bubble-gum-pink keloids like he'd packed it with Bazooka. Fog condensed on his gray stubble. He wore a sailor cap. Its tally bore the letters "S. S. TANGO."

Willie looked away. He'd been staring long enough. He didn't dare meet the man's gaze. Willie slinked along the gunwale toward the stern and watched the lights along the shoreline dimming off. Sunrise scrubbed through distant clouds, leaving glimmers on the swells rising and falling atop a sultry surging sea.

Undulations tossed the boat. Lifted the taxi like an elevator up and then released it. Two more waves came in their wake. The boat splashed down. New swells seemed larger, and they left an empty spot in Willie's stomach.

The jack-of-diamonds man give Willie a cold stare.

Red sky at morning. Willie shuddered. He recalled the four-line ditty from third grade and hoped the lyrics wouldn't wind up coming true. The *Tango* nodded in the distance, and Willie wondered if the swells were strong enough to topple stacked-up decks of playing cards at crap tables or chips on their roulette table. His gut told him rough weather was en-route. *Sailors take warning.*

The sun rose through a cloud on the horizon.

The taxi puttered forward toward the portside of the *Tango.* Workers tied it to the lower deck, extending a steel gangway to the taxi from the boarding deck. Tunes blared from tinny loudspeakers. Willie recognized the music, *Pennies from Heaven*. Eddie Duchin. Upstairs, Willie smelled alcohol, tobacco smoke, and perfume.

Men in black nautical sportcoats helped three ladies wearing fox stoles from the taxi. Two wooden staircases ascended up from both sides of the boarding deck. Willie followed the tattooed stranger to the gambling deck upstairs, taking care to stay a dozen steps below him.

And then it struck him – Suicide Jack, the man José had talked about, Loretta's friend. Willie glanced back at the tattoo on his shipmate. There were such cards as suicide kings, but suicide *jacks*? He felt uneasy.

He let a passenger slip between him and the man with the tattoo.

He swallowed hard, having a hunch the man would lead him to Loretta. He'd need to follow Jack upstairs while still remaining undetected. The tattooed eye spilling out blood seemed to be staring back at Willie.

The sound of slot machines ahead in the casino jarred his nerves.

Below the gambling deck, the crew pulled in the gangway from the water taxi. Planks telescoped inward. The taxi crew changed out the number boards, so Water Taxi 8 changed into Water Taxi 12, returning home from "Catalina" within a realistic timeframe. It was their alibi, thought Willie, and it helped to keep the books straight since round trips to Catalina would require several hours. The water taxi motored back to Newport with five passengers and sputtered down the coast toward Orange County.

It seemed everyone aboard the *S.S. Tango* knew the trick. The gamblers laughed about it. Added to the ambiance and intrigue, people said. They seemed to feel as if their ship had put one over on the law, given that Buron Fitts, the Los Angeles County District Attorney, had decided water taxis to gambling ships should be illegal in his effort to put gambling ships and barges out of business.

Suicide Jack slipped through the crowd. Willie moved to remain close, dodging a trio of old women wearing Greta Garbo cloche hats. He made his way between a pair of double doors into a banquet room with oriental carpeting and fifteen well-worn crap tables.

Then Willie saw her. Loretta wore a perky red beret above a velvet strapless evening gown displaying all her assets. She held a tray of cigarettes inside a varnished wooden box that said, "Old Gold". He'd never seen her in high heels.

She hadn't spied him yet. It helped that Willie wasn't supposed to be here. Suicide Jack moved her direction, smacked a kiss on her left cheek and said, "Hullo, toots." Loretta raised her chin to look away, and then her gaze landed on....

...Willie.

Willie froze.

The air in the casino instantly felt air-conditioned. He fought to breathe. Loretta glared at him from thirty feet away. Her panic-stricken face telegraphed her rising anger. Willie almost thought he saw her mouth the words, "You shouldn't be here," except Loretta's lips weren't moving. She stood there statuelike, as pale as white marble, painted fingernails shaking as the chill from off the ocean seemed to swallow the casino.

"What is it, dollcakes?" Jack inquired.

"I just saw someone I know."

"Want me to talk to him? Where is he?"

"Please," Loretta said. "Please don't."

"He's over there. I saw you staring."

Willie tried to duck away, except Loretta's gaze was tracking him. She fired him a look. There was no way to escape. Suicide Jack had spotted Willie and crossed his arms, flexing his muscle so the knife inside the jack of diamonds' eye wiggled around.

Willie glanced around the room, looking for some way to escape.

Jack gestured with his fingertips for Willie to come forward.

Willie walked toward Loretta. His heart was racing, rattling faster than a Thompson submachine gun. He took a breath, stuck out his chest, and bit his lip to quell anxiety, glancing toward a bouncer in the corner whom he hoped might guarantee things didn't escalate.

"So, you found me," said Loretta. "Might I ask what it's about? I'm on the clock right now."

"I had myself a chat with Larry Norton." Willie said.

Loretta blanched. He was surprised Suicide Jack now interrupted. "Dollcakes, is this about Elena?"

Loretta's gaze darted about, and she stepped back.

Willie said, "Yes."

Startled, Loretta glared at Jack. She jabbed her thumb over her shoulder toward the doorway to the deck. Her smile felt colder than the room. She turned toward Jack. Their gazes locked, almost as if they were conversing. The stares continued thirty seconds, and Jack's face was turning red. "Hit the trail, killer whale," Loretta finally blurted out. Willie swallowed his surprise that Jack obeyed.

Willie still shivered.

And Loretta's scowl could freeze him in his steps.

CHAPTER XII

ABOARD THE *S.S. TANGO*, MONDAY, MARCH 28

The morning sky had turned to scarlet, and the ocean now felt choppy. Huge waves banged against the hull, and thunderbolts lit the horizon. A monster wave lifted the ship. The *Tango* lurched hard to the starboard. Willie was thrown against a gambling table, bruising his left thigh. Gambling chips spilled off roulette tables and tumbled to the deck. A shriek. A woman in a pleated gray skirt knelt to pick her chips up. More swells slammed against the ship. Poker chips rattled to the floor, and all the gamblers raked their winnings into paper sacks and purses and were moving toward the exits.

Willie surveyed the casino.

Suicide Jack stepped through a pair of double doors off to the starboard. He glanced once over his shoulder. Men in dinner jackets came. "We'll need to shut down the casino." Passengers swallowed down their drinks, gathering all of their belongings, snuffing cigars and cigarettes out, making beelines toward the exits.

Then the lights went out. The rumbling diesel engines had gone silent. The *S. S. Tango* had lost power. Murmurs filled the dark casino. It was gray outside and even darker inside the casino. Clouds were dumping sheets of rain onto the deck. The gamblers muttered. Apparently, a bolt of lightning had struck somewhere near the bow. Those who'd made their way outside staggered back in to find some cover.

Loretta tugged on Willie's wrist. She led him out of the casino to a hallway lined with gas lanterns and rows of wooden doors. She had a room key to a tiny little cabin on the starboard. The key scraped inside the lock.

The door flung open.

Willie entered. Loretta followed him inside and locked the cabin door. She gave Willie a shove, and he collapsed onto her bedspread.

"What are you doing here?" she asked, folding her arms across her chest.

Willie stared up at Loretta and took in the tiny cabin.

Not much in here, he concluded. There was her ugly leather suitcase, brown cordovan; dirty clothes and a cloth case containing toiletries. It sat beside the sink beneath a water-spotted mirror.

Willie glared at her and frowned. "You never said you had three daughters."

"Does it matter?" she fired back. She wore a shiny-beaded necklace that she toyed with when she wasn't tugging silvery hoop earrings.

"You said Elena was your sister."

"So?" Loretta scowled and shoved her hands against her hips. She cocked her chin. "I've tried to help you. Is this all the thanks

I get, you little mick? Why are you bringing this up now? This is not the place or time," Loretta said. Again her hands went to her earrings then returned down to the necklace like she had to finger something when not smoking.

Willie waited. He let a long minute of silence calm Loretta. His heart stopped pounding. "Because I cared about Elena," Willie said. "Which means I care about your family. Enough to visit Mister Norton at his farmhouse, a man I gather isn't fit to be your friend."

Loretta's jaw dropped. "You saw Norton?" Both her hands moved to her chest.

Willie nodded. "So, who's *Abuelo*?" Willie asked." He's not your grandfather. Norton talked more than he should have, so don't lie. I know the truth. I've learned a few things I should tell you. I also think I've earned the right to hear your side of things but not to have to put up with more lies."

"He's my father," said Loretta.

Willie looked down at the floor. "I was afraid of that," he said. "I have some devastating news."

She touched his shoulder. Her touch felt tentative and trembling, like she thought she could control him, but she almost seemed to fear she might not want to. Her eyes widened. Loretta looked him in the eye and whispered, "Tell me."

"He...."

Loretta whimpered, *"Ay, Dios mío. Es verdad."* She found a Kleenex in her handbag. Dabbed her eyelids. Looked away. Crumpled the tissue in her fist and threw it down, crying, *"Mi padre...."*

"Yes," said Willie. He reached to touch her, but Loretta pulled away.

Loretta managed to stay calm. Looked at him. Whispered, *"¿Es muerto?"*

Willie nodded. He let Loretta wrap her mind around the horror that her father and her daughter had both died. It was hard not to feel pity. The loss of so much family in one flood. So much cruelty and hatred at the hands of those who used her. She held her sterling sliver necklace almost like it was a Rosary and tugged its lower end across her heart.

Willie told her how Elena had described *abuelo's* drowning in the torrent of the Santa Ana River in the deluge, how she'd asked Norton for help, how she'd been thrown onto the street, how José had said the coroner thought Elena had been raped.

"I paid that bastard," said Loretta. "Eighty dollars every month went to the Nortons."

"The bastard part would be correct," Willie replied. "I beat him up. Beat him up good. Had to do it for Elena."

Loretta eyes were leaking tears. Then she seemed to turn to steel. Her jaw set firm, and she looked wound up even tighter than his wristwatch.

Willie felt his own eyes dampen. "I've told you everything I know, Loretta. Everything. I clobbered Norton. Put him in the hospital."

Loretta gave him an odd look, like she was happy, but she didn't dare admit it. Willie hoped he had convinced her not to lie. He needed help, and he'd just proven he could penetrate her smokescreen. He hoped Loretta understood now it would pay her to cooperate.

"I thought he'd raped Elena," Willie said. "But now I'm not so sure, and I'd be grateful if you told me just the truth from here on out."

She met his gaze. And for a change her pupils didn't look like bullets. It was the first time he had found a way to peer beyond her hardness. Except by now he didn't trust her. He never should have to begin with. Still, he needed her. She knew the sorts of things nice folks won't ask about. Sometimes you have to tunnel underneath the nice to find the truth. It was a skill Loretta'd mastered, a skill he'd started to admire.

He asked her, "Who's Elena's father?" He grabbed her arm and gave a squeeze, feeling the heartbeat through her flesh telling him she was upset too.

Loretta wiped off her mascara. "A little knowledge might be dangerous."

Willie's palm slammed hard against her bed table.

Loretta blushed. She looked away. Even the storm outside had mellowed. She was staring at his wristwatch.

Willie caught her.

She looked up. And then she slowly turned her head again and stared back at his watch and said, "My husband." Sweat was pouring down her face. Or was it tears?

Willie's mind spun with a whirlpool of emotions.

She'd never mentioned she'd been married. Things were starting to make sense, but he had questions. "Why did he leave if he had you, and he had money?" Willie asked. "Something says a man would want to stick around."

Loretta sat down on her bed. "That Elgin wristwatch on your arm." She touched it like a child strokes a sickly little bird. "Your 'lucky wristwatch" from Elena. It was her father's watch. I bought it."

Willie breathed in deep and looked outside.

Rain reappeared on the horizon.

She rose again and looked at Willie. "For his birthday. It was supposed to bring him luck, only it didn't. Or it only brought him luck until he left it on the bedstand."

It heartened him her story at least matched up with Elena's.

A flash of light lit up the porthole, followed by a clap of thunder. The sea swelled like a thousand tons of rage, heaving the ship, and hard rain hammered on the cabin walls like never-ending birdshot.

Another bolt of lightning lit the room.

"I hope the water taxi makes it back to Newport," said Loretta. "If it does, they won't be coming back real soon." She looked outside.

Willie stood up from the bed. He touched Loretta on her chin and nudged her gaze back toward his own. "I need to know about your husband. Elena never said that much about him."

"Javy was murdered," said Loretta.

Murdered? It was not something that Willie was prepared for. She'd said it so matter-of-factly, like it didn't even faze her. Her cozy cabin felt cold as an ice cave.

"*Güeros* killed Mexicans back then. They'd disappear. People would say they were deported. But you *gringos* don't know jack about those days."

"I'm not 'you *gringos*,' *No soy güero*. I'm part Mexican like you." Willie's fist pounded the bedspread.

"You're still part-Irish," said Loretta, looking off toward her mirror.

"So, what about it? I'm sure as hades not old money from New England. Aren't the *San Patricios* both Irish and Mexican?" he stammered. "They joined your side and fought off Grant at Churubusco."

"You grew up white. We call it 'passing.'" A callous smile.

"Right now, I'm homeless," Willie said.

"So am I," fired back Loretta, shaking out her head of hair. "You think I like this crummy gig? Shacked up in Tony's little whorehouse on the mainland? Lighting cigarettes for nasty, leering *güeros* on his boats. You think...."

"You haven't told me where your husband died," said Willie.

Loretta's pupils narrowed back to bullets.

She hunted down a cigarette. "Javy died right on this ship,"

Willie felt sick.

She lit her Marlboro. Inhaled deep. Seemed to relax. Glanced toward the ceiling. "He won big at the roulette table." Her voice cracked like she didn't want to tell. "We'd hit hard times. Lost our apartment in L.A. He'd made good money in the slaughterhouses. Cudahy had hired him in his teens. But the Depression came. White people needed jobs, so he got fired by the stockyards." Loretta tugged on her left earring. Said we were lucky they didn't ship him back to Mexico with the others. But he was born in Santa Ana, and he didn't want to leave." She grabbed her necklace. "So Javy gambled. Plopped down all of his life savings on double-zero, and he won. Did it again. He won again. Twice in a row. What are the odds? Walked off with eighteen-thousand dollars worth of poker chips. He went to the cashier to cash them in."

Willie stepped toward the porthole. He saw Loretta's face reflected in the glass. She tugged an earring off and set it on the table. Then she removed her other earring and was fiddling with her necklace, and her voice dropped half an octave when she got to the next part.

"But he was Mexican. It was cheaper to have bouncers throw him overboard. Can't even prove the man got born unless they sift through all our church records. And who does that? They split our eighteen-thousand dollars with the ship. Javy washed up on the shore on Seal Beach just like Elena. Funny," Loretta said, her gaze turned toward Willie, and she frowned. "What were the odds they'd both wash up on the same beach?" She rubbed her chin.

"What are the odds of hitting double-zero twice?" Willie replied. He exhaled and the glass steamed with his breath. He turned around. But why would someone like Loretta work for people who had murdered her own husband. Willie finger-drummed the bed table.

She set her Marlboro in the ashtray. "What the hell else could I do? I knew enough I could shut down their operation and their ship, except it seems like I'm not white. Who the hell listens to a greaser with big tits who's unemployed? I did exactly what I had to. I suggested that they hire me. Said I had pictures in a safe deposit box in Santa Ana. That got Tony to take notice. He knew my husband had been murdered, and he didn't want publicity. I said if anything unfortunate should happen to my family, the heat would find the safe deposit key and scoot down to the bank. I told them everything that D.A. Buron Fitts has ever dreamed about was right inside my safe deposit box for his enjoyment."

"So, were you bluffing?"

"Suppose I was? Seemed Tony didn't like those odds."

"Isn't that blackmail?"

"It's business. Lousy bastards killed my husband." Loretta reached into her suitcase. Grabbed another cigarette.

Willie made his way across the cabin.

Loretta found a matchbook, struck a match, and lit her Marlboro.

"Tony Cornero understands me. Tony the Hat, you know? The Admiral. He stares at me. He says, 'So what's your ask?' He looks away.

"I say 'Right now I got no husband. I have three daughters nine through thirteen years of age. And all you need to do is see I stay employed, and I'll stay mum.

"'Mexican standoff?' Tony laughed at his own joke.

"'*Exactamente.* Just keep me happy. Pay me enough that I can take care of my daughters, and I'll make it worth your while to employ me.'

"So, he does. Tony Cornero shakes my hand. We got a deal. He even brings me to Las Vegas, lets me sleep inside his dive in Santa Ana. And so, it seems we have a mutual agreement until *La Migra* goons cart both Elena's sisters to Sonora. I pay Norton up in Atwood to look after my old man and my last daughter. But he welches on the deal when the floods come. That's about the time you walked into the movie, I recall." She looked up." *¿Comprende?*" Her gaze landed on Willie.

Willie nodded.

It was a convoluted story, but it seemed to piece together. The lights flickered. Went on, then off, then sputtered back to life, but somewhat dimmer. The slot machines came jingling back to life.

"Backup genset in the boiler room," Loretta said. "We done? Even my boyfriend doesn't know half what I told you."

"Suicide Jack?"

"Some call him that. Right now, I need to change my clothes." Loretta said. She made her way toward the sink, and she set down her cigarette.

"I'm mighty sorry," Willie said. "About your father. If it helps."

She grabbed his hand. Sandwiched it in-between her palms and said, "You're sweet. I'm kinda sad I never saw you with Elena."

"Me too," said Willie. "We could use a little sweetness in our lives."

Loretta nodded.

He was surprised she even knew the word for sweet.

Willie steeled himself, rose, and made his way into the corridor, closing the cabin door behind him. He wandered back toward the casino. There were still unanswered questions, but he knew more than he had. He made a vow someone would pay for what had happened to Elena just as soon as he could find out who'd defiled his dead lover.

Willie walked through the casino doors. The lights hit him like several hundred flash bulbs; the noise made Willie's head feel like a pinball. His thoughts whirled like a carousel had switched into high gear. He didn't like it here. He wondered how Loretta could endure it. He wanted nothing more than to sail home.

Someone tapped Willie on the shoulder. The man's breath reeked of sour tobacco. Willie turned around. Suicide Jack stood there to meet him. The sailor didn't seem too happy. His face was creased into a scowl. He was the last person that Willie cared to see right at the moment.

Jack spat snuff onto the deck. The man was Willie's height but built like Caterpillar tractors construction workers graded dams with. Willie glared into Jack's face. Right now, a fuse seemed to be lit, and the man's temper was approaching detonation.

His lantern bulldozer-shaped jaw looked wide enough to blade a roadway. He crossed his arms. They looked like legs and nearly ripped open his shirtsleeves. He cornered Willie, backed him up against a mirrored cigarette machine. He breathed in Willie's face and blurted, "Who the hell are you?"

His voice surprised Willie. High and shrill, it didn't match the build at all, made Willie think Jack had been bullied and mailed in money to Charles Atlas. But the results were right in front of Willie. Snarling. With a grudge.

Willie stood his ground. "Elena's boyfriend."

Jack took a step back. Something about Elena's name seemed to upset the man. A lot. He folded both his arms in front of him. "You know Elena?" *That tenor voice*.

"*Knew* Elena," Willie said.

Suicide Jack showed no reaction. He glanced over both his shoulders. Then he smirked. "Little birdie sez you've shacked up with Loretta."

"I'm a virgin," Willie deadpanned, looking straight into Jack's eye, trying to imagine he still was. He didn't dare to look away. He wasn't any good at lying, but he dared not tell the truth.

Jack's upper lip curled in a condescending sneer.

Jack rolled up his sleeves. Flexed his forearm muscles. Frowned. "I'm not so sure, you little shit."

Willie stared at that tattoo.

Jack tensed his forearms, and the flesh rolled. "I find out you rang her bell...." Both forearms twitched. Jack touched his middle finger to the jack of diamonds' eye. "Get the picture, turdbreath?"

Shudders crawled through Willy.

"Smack-dab in the eyeball." Willie expected him to laugh. He jabbed his thumb toward Willie's eye. Thumped his fist against his palm. Then he just stared at Willie, chewing on a wad of snuff the size of an old golf ball.

Willie saw bouncers just a dozen feet a way.

Jack hocked his wad of snuff at Willie. It landed on his shirt.

He nearly gagged. The stain oozed down the front between

the buttons, and it reeked. Willie stepped back. This was not the time or place to pick a fight.

Jack walked away, clapping his hands together, not turning around.

There was Loretta. She spun to face Jack, and he kissed her on the lips.

Willie rushed from the casino, his stomach turning inside-out. He found a restroom. Toweled his shirt off. Lathered saltwater all over it. Scrubbed the stain away the best he could. A brown spot still remained. He'd spent two dollars on a Sanforized white-collar button Arrow shirt, and Jack had gone and ruined it. He wondered what Loretta saw in Jack.

Willie returned to the casino. It felt colder than a meat locker. Toward the stern he saw a water taxi out of Seal Beach. He thought of it as an investment, get the hell off of the *Tango*. It wasn't safe out here. Jack worked on-board and couldn't leave the ship, but Willie *could*. He wasn't welcome. Time to buy a ticket.

But there was no charge for returning water taxis. The *Tango* made their money on the gambling. Willie climbed aboard the taxi with three couples. A slender woman in a day dress bragged she'd won two-hundred dollars. Willie moved up near the bow, straightened a seat cushion, sat down, and heard the water taxi motor on its way back to the shore.

He'd learned a lot. He had confirmed Elena's mother was Loretta, learned her father had been murdered, learned how Loretta made her money, had met her scary boyfriend, Jack, who seemed to live onboard the Tango, making his Charlie Boards and selling them to Rico back onshore.

Willie felt cold. A tailwind off the ocean chilled his neck, reminding Willie he still didn't have a clue who'd raped Elena.

CHAPTER XIII

SANTA ANA: WEDNESDAY, APRIL 6

From Page 1 of *The Santa Ana Register*

PLACENTIA ORCHARDMAN DIES AT ORANGE COUNTY GENERAL.

Santa Ana, California: Sheriffs report 44-year-old Placentia businessman and farmer, Lawrence Richard Norton, who was assaulted by vagrant Mexicans two weeks ago outside his Placentia farmhouse, has died from complications resulting from massive internal injuries suffered as a result of the attack. The Orange County Sheriff's Department has expanded their investigation, now for murder. The suspect is believed to be a six-foot teen-age Mexican who is thought to have been spotted wearing a Hollywood Stars baseball cap. The hat was found discarded in a ditch outside the property.

Norton's widow, Priscilla, claims the man had stalked her house and might have also been associated with the murder and rape of 17-year-old Elena Valenzuela, whose mutilated corpse was found last month at Seal Beach. Those with knowledge of people trespassing in the vicinity of Norton's property are urged by the County Sheriff's Office to contact the Department. A reward is being offered by the widow, Priscilla Norton. Deputies have been added to the expanded investigation.

The morning sun glared off the sheet glass on the store fronts facing Main Street, and the smell of eggs and bacon made its way outside the Woolworth's. Willie stared down at the newsrack at the corner of Fifth and Main.

His heart stopped.

What the hell? The front-page news on Norton shocked him.

He bought a copy. Tucked it underneath his armpit, walked a block. He'd make a right turn up at Olive Street. He hadn't seen Loretta since the *Tango*. Willie was worried. Suicide Jack made Willie fear about her safety.

And now this.

Plus, Mildred Kent might rat him out.

Somehow the whole thing had blown up. Norton never should have died. You didn't die from a concussion or a pair of broken ribs. That was absurd. And if you did, you didn't wait a couple weeks, *then* kick the bucket. Something was fishy. Willie knew it in his gut. But nobody would listen to a "six-foot teen-age Mexican" who'd stared down Mrs. Norton and her shotgun only weeks ago. Willie wondered why he even bothered staying in Orange County. But where else could he go? And ever since Elena's murder, he'd been antsy to seek justice for his girl.

Maybe José down at the barbershop would know a thing or two. José's friend worked at the coroner's. He'd known Elena had been raped, stuff the news never reported. Perhaps José could help. Plus, the man owed him after finding him those Charlie Boards. He'd probably cashed in now and made several hundred dollars.

There was a crosswalk up on Flower Street. The man crossing the street looked like an icebox that had legs. He wore a sailor's cap. *Oh crap!*

Willie froze right in his steps and watched the man cross to the southern side of Fifth Street.

Suicide Jack.

This time he wasn't with Loretta.

Willie followed, a block behind, maintaining distance to make sure he wasn't noticed. Suicide Jack ambled the two blocks south to Third Street. From there Jack walked another block, pausing just outside José's.

Suicide Jack glanced at his notes and stepped inside of José's barbershop.

Willie turned and walked away. Best to eat lunch down at the Woolworth's and avoid a confrontation. This was not the time or place. Only he had a nasty feeling he'd run into Jack again.

He didn't want to.

But sometimes people didn't get their wish.

CHAPTER XIV

SANTA ANA: SATURDAY, APRIL 9

For three days, Willie had lain low, snooping around in Santa Ana for any clues about Elena. So far Willie'd come up empty. He'd even gone to the police. Used a fake Italian name, scared to death some cop would notice he was *six feet tall and Mexican,* same description they had used for Norton's killer in the *Register*. The trip downtown proved uneventful. Willie didn't learn a thing. No one cared about Elena, and no one noticed Willie looked just like the sketch of Norton's "killer." Willie counted himself lucky. He didn't care to take more chances with the law.

It had been a wasted gamble. Still no word out of Loretta. Willie hoped that she was safe. He feared something had happened since he hadn't even seen her. Like himself, perhaps she wanted to avoid Suicide Jack, who knew her address. Willie did not want Jack to know that Willie lived there. And so he'd stayed out of the house and kept the doors locked, just in case Jack left the *Tango* and came onshore for a visit to Loretta's.

But time was passing. Willie needed information from José's friend at the coroner's on anomalies of Mr. Norton's death. So much about it seemed suspicious, and the newspapers had lied. He had to find some things out for himself.

He entered José's barbershop. The cowbell clanked behind him. Customers read comic books and waited for their turn. Jose was finishing a buzzcut on a fourteen-year-old boy when he saw Willie.

José's face became a scowl.

"You need a haircut?" snapped José, showing puzzling hostility.

"No, I just stopped...."

"Let's step outside." He yanked his thumb over his shoulder. He said, "Excuse us," to the boy who sat and read *Detective Comics*.

Willie felt his stomach knot and stepped outside behind José into the alley. The man looked furious. Willie asked, "So what's the deal?"

"Willie, I don't need no more Charley Boards. Not ever." José sputtered.

"Jeez, what hap...?"

José's hands balled into fists. He looked away. Spat in the gravel. "People know the winning squares. I check it out." He shook his fist. "Squares are the same on every Charlie Board in town. Each one's identical."

"What?"

"They're a scam. Even the cops know all about them, but don't do diddly. Say it's an object lesson on why we shouldn't gamble. Lazy scumbags. Whoever manufactures Charley Boards has more than one confederate. These guys are working all

Orange County, cleaning out the winning numbers on every Charley Board in town."

"But that's impossible."

"You think? Lost me one-hundred-fifty bucks, all before noon. Guy pays me two bits and a dollar. Walks off with twenty-five simoleons. It's rigged. Loretta's friend Suicide Jack walks in three days ago and walks away with fifty-seven bucks after five minutes. Every square he bets on pays him off."

Willie felt sick to learn that Jack was playing both sides of the deal, collecting cash for making boards then cleaning out the winning squares. His temples felt like they could pop. Suicide Jack had double-crossed him, undercutting Willie's friend. He didn't have that many allies. Plus he depended on José for information from the coroner. Which meant he couldn't even find out what went on with Mr. Norton. Unless....

Willie rubbed his chin. Pulled out a twenty from his wallet. "Suppose I help reduce your losses." Willie showed José the twenty.

"And what is this for?"

"Information. Your nurse friend at the coroner's downtown. I need the scoop on this guy Norton. How he died."

"You mean that redneck some guy poisoned."

Willie took a breath. "How do you know about this stuff? The papers never say a word."

"Nicky gets pretty upset. Hospitals coverin' stuff up."

"Why would they do that?" Willie asked.

"This guy has *ricin* in his system. You cook the castor beans that grow on local plants to make the poison. It didn't get there by mistake. The hospitals in town don't want no lawsuits for gross negligence."

"So he was...."

"Murdered," said José. "Whoever puts him in the hospital comes back to finish up."

Willie took a huge step back. He'd seen the plant back at Loretta's place and somebody had harvested the beans. It had seemed odd.

"How do you know Norton was poisoned?"

"Ain't it obvious?" José looked up and shrugged. "Why do you care about this crap? Leave it alone." He rolled his eyes. "You'd be minding your own beeswax if you're smart."

Murdered? The word was echoing inside of Willie's brain. It disappointed him how everybody covered up their backs, telling the public outright lies, anything to keep their noses clean, oblivious that somebody like Willie paid the price if the police found out he'd had that fight with Norton.

But there was somebody behind this. Willie counted up his enemies. Mildred was a monster but knew nothing about Norton. Maybe Enrico had a beef with him since Willie owed him money, or Suicide Jack, but how would Jack know anything about Elena? Or it could even be Loretta.

Willie's mind was spinning.

He knew that he would need to find out quick to stay alive.

Worried sick, Willie walked home. He wondered what he might do now. Any day, he feared the cops would come and haul him off for questioning, all to keep Orange County General protected from a lawsuit after somebody had slipped inside to poison old man Norton.

To make it worse, he knew his days of selling Charlie Boards were through. The sort of folks who ran Orange County liked to look the other way when there was crime. Make things look nicey-nice and cover up the details. That helped criminals, but honest people paid for their indifference. The law didn't give a damn. Their silence benefited crooks when there were so many outsiders for the cops to pin the blame on.

And clearly half-breeds such as Willie were outsiders.

Footsteps padded ahead of Willie. He glanced ahead to see a mutt wagging his tail, making his way around a wino on the sidewalk. The mutt sniffed the old man's trousers, looked away, and jogged toward Willie. Sniffed Willie's knees, his shoes, his hand, and started licking.

He was a ragged little pup, but he was sweet in his own way. The brick-brown hair on the dog's legs was tied in greasy mats of fur which felt like peanuts when you rubbed them. They were filthy to the touch. Wiilie wondered where he slept, clearly somewhere on the street. Pup wagged his tail again, and Willie gave the dog a bite of jerky.

The mutt snarfed down the food and trotted off into an alley. He seemed so happy. Willie hoped in his next life he'd be a dog. Willie stepped over the wino and continued on his way, wishing people were as innocent as animals.

After an interlude of sweetness, Willie pushed away the memories of dogs, of Elena's lingering kisses, of her smile. It was time to go to work, and Josefina would be furious.

Making his way toward Loretta's, Willie noticed something missing.

Behind the prickly pears, the *chollas*, and the bathtub Virgin Mary, by the hose bibb was a dirt pile where the castor bean had been. The plant was *gone*. Almost like somebody had dug it up on purpose to hide evidence the bean plant had been harvested.

He shivered. *Coincidence?* Willie had his doubts. Besides himself, only three people had the keys to Tony's place.

That meant he knew Norton's killer, either Loretta, Jack, or Tony, although nobody could prove which one had done it.

He was also odd man out, not to mention the prime suspect. Most of the evidence was pointing straight at Willie. It occurred to him that now he knew too much. His heart accelerated. Someone had framed Willie for the death.of Lawrence Norton.

Which meant they might have planted evidence already.

Five minutes later, Willie caught his breath outside of Josefina's. He was late. His heart raced faster than a hot Chicago typewriter. He made his way through the front door to enter Josefina's dining room. It usually felt warm.

It didn't now.

The floor was coated with fresh sawdust, but it badly needed mopping. Nobody greeted him today, not that people ever did. Most of the workers didn't like him, since he "passed" for being Anglo. One of the busboys from the kitchen studied Willie up and down, jerked his chin, then glanced at Willie. "You need to step into the kitchen."

"Huh?"

"Rosalita wants to see you." The busboy smirked, and Willie's stomach twisted, tightening enough to stop his breath.

He walked slowly, dreading somebody had knifed him in the back while he'd been gone. From the moment he set foot inside the galley it was obvious his instincts were correct.

"Where were you Wednesday, you lazy *rubio?*" Rosalita was a niece of Josefina's and was livid. "Nobody here knew where you were. You never called us."

"I was, uh, sick."

"Were you so weak you couldn't phone us? Stuck in an iron lung with polio? On your deathbed?"

"It was my fault, and I'm sorry."

"Oh, please spare us the apology. No one likes you here. You're lazy. You don't carry your own weight."

Willie swallowed back his words. He couldn't tell the real truth about the trouble he was in.

He saw the whole kitchen was listening.

"You're fired, Willie. See that door." Rosalita snapped her fingers. "Don't let it slap you in the ass." Grinning, she pointed toward the exit.

Blood raced into Willie's temples, but he swallowed back his anger. It was already a bad day after his visit with José, after he'd figured out that somebody he knew was trying to frame him for a murder. Now he'd been *canned*. His whole life had come unraveled. He'd need to make a call to Rico, learn what he could about Loretta, maybe hunt down another job or find out who had rigged the Charlie Boards. He noticed how the Mexicans seemed glad to see him fired. As if he wasn't one of them. Except he wasn't one of anything. He was "passing," too white for Mexicans, too brown to be an Anglo, the perfect color to piss everybody off.

He made his way from Josefina's. Didn't even slam the door. He closed it softly, hoping irony might send a subtler message.

There was a phone booth a block east. Willie opened the glass doors and dropped a nickel.

Dialed Enrico. He wasn't quite sure what to say.

The phone rang. Five rings. Ten.

Twelve Rings. Willie's heart hammered.

At last a woman's voice picked up.

Willie asked, "Enrico home?"

"Enrico who?"

"I owe him money."

"All I can say is he don't live here."

"When did he leave?"

"He didn't leave. He just don't live here. Anymore." Willie heard tears over the phone. The woman clearly was upset.

Willie thought to ask if Rico might have been Loretta's handler but decided some discretion was the better part of valor. Enrico'd split. There was his answer. Everything Willie had to know. Evidently Rico's business had seen some sort of reversal. Willie asked, "Rico say anything about a guy named Jack?"

There was a long nerve-racking silence. Then she whispered. "Jack Malone? You ever say that bastard's name again, I call the bloody heat. Or ain't you wise that he killed Rico? Ran a dagger through his *eyeball*. Who in bloody God's green Hades are you?"

Willie's jaw dropped like a giant slug of lead. "I was just ask...."

A dial tone.

Damn it. Willie slammed the phone down.

He had no job. And Mildred Kent had cut his legs out from beneath him. José was livid. Rico, Norton, and Elena were all dead. Suicide Jack had made that threat to knife him "smack-dab in the eyeball." And Willie feared that any day Orange County's sheriff would come calling. He felt "screwed, blued, and tattooed," as old man Stanley used to say.

But he hadn't killed a soul. He was just trying to solve a murder.

He longed to get out of Orange County. Ride the *Sunset* to Arizona or the *Lark* to San Francisco, someplace nobody would know him. But he'd still be what he was. *Cholo* was written on his skin. Lousy odds if he stayed put and maybe worse if he split town. There were three strong possibilities on who had poisoned Norton. Willie shuddered.

And all of them had worked out on the *Tango.*

He knew the odds. He'd like to settle up with Jack and with Loretta. It was his way to help Elena. Not that anybody cared, but she had loved him. And her love deserved devotion, especially now that she'd been murdered.

He walked a mile and a half down to the Santa Ana depot. There he waited twenty minutes for the next trolley to Huntington. The Red Car rumbled south to Dyer where it passed south of the sugar plant, and chilly ocean breezes made their way off Newport Bay. Signs passed for Bristol, Greenville, Talbert. Willie's heart rose in his throat. Was he doing the right thing, or had he crossed over to crazy like Loretta had and Jack? That was how foxes stayed alive. He swallowed hard and sucked his cheeks in. The sun was sinking into beanfields. Willie had no reservation on the *Tango* for tonight. But this way no one would suspect him. He could show up to surprise them.

The trolley made a hard turn to the left.

South to Bushard, west to Thompsonville. The car zigzagged toward Huntington. Willie thought he saw the *Tango's* silhouette out on the water. The Red Car rolled along the shore past Tin Can Beach. The sun was setting.

"Anaheim Landing," the conductor called. The last stop before Willie's.

The sun slipped over the horizon.

"Seal Beach."

He tugged the chord.

Cars and motorcycles were parked along a mile of Coast Highway. Neon signs were lighting up for all the nightclubs.

Asbestos brakes burned, and sparks flickered from the pantograph above. Steel wheels groaned. The Red Car slowed and crawled up toward the depot.

"Seal Beach. This here's your stop." The conductor jerked a thumb over his shoulder, and Willie exited the Red Car's steel steps. He wondered what he'd wear tomorrow, not having a suitcase.

He set his jaw.

A group of sailors lined up outside a casino.

Only a few blocks to the water taxis leaving from the pier.

Sparks on the pantograph returned, and Willie stared out from the platform as the Red Car rumbled northwest toward Long Beach.

He'd need to do this for Elena. Or maybe do it for himself. He needed vengeance. The very thought of Suicide Jack made Willie's blood boil.

He'd find a place to sleep tonight.

He'd leave tomorrow for the *Tango*.

He set his jaw. From here on out, he'd fight alone.

CHAPTER XV

SEAL BEACH: MONDAY, APRIL 11

Willie knew of Seal Beach's reputation as "Sin City." The town was custom-made for sailors who found Long Beach far too boring. Unlike Long Beach, or as sailors called it, "Iowa-by-the-Sea," where one-hundred-fifty-thousand staid Midwesterners had settled, Seal Beach, reigned as the "pleasure place" with everything a sailor ever dreamed of, an "open city" where the laws were not enforced: gambling, bawdy houses, bathing beauties, night swims, big band orchestras, and incandescent lights along the boardwalk and the pier, famed as the second longest jetty in California.

Lonely, Willie walked down Main Street past the lights of the Beach Theater. *Jezebel* was showing with Bette Davis and Henry Fonda. Lines of busty girls in bathing suits were huddled near the entrance, smoking cigarettes, and making themselves known to local sailors.

Ahead, the last rays of the sunset disappeared behind an old abandoned roller coaster, a remnant of the Roaring Twenties Jewel Café and "Joy Zone." Offshore, the *Show-Boat*, another local offshore gambling ship was shuttling back and forth between the waters of Orange County and L. A. County. County sheriffs were obliged to stay within their jurisdictions, allowing ship captains to dodge the law by moving into waters where the law enforcers didn't have authority. The *Show-Boat* could change jurisdictions every fifteen minutes.

Willie turned and headed north. He was following the crowds who staggered inland from the beaches to the clubs along Coast Highway. Printed flyers, tacked to casinos, advertised the local nightclubs. Starting at seven, there was a concert at Vivian Laird's Garden of Allah, corner of 8th Street and Coast Highway. Jack Teagarden was playing. A night of dancing might be just what Willie needed to pick his spirits up, meet some doll to take his mind off all his troubles.

He crossed Electric Avenue's trolley tracks. Neon lights glowed up ahead along Coast Highway. Glid'er Inn, Dovalis Ranch House, Coast Inn Coffee Shop. To his left, Vivian Laird's Garden of Allah lit the night. Long lines had already formed outside.

It seemed several hundred sailors, out on shore leave from their ships, had headed down the coast from Long Beach. And there were just as many women.

Willie walked along the south edge of the highway on the shoulder.

A motorcar pulled onto the gravel, stopped, and headlights blazed behind him, lit the night up like a theater marquee. A car horn honked.

It honked again, and Willie turned.

At the wheel of Rico's Auburn sat Loretta.

She smiled at Willie. Cleared her throat and shook her hair out. She'd put the top down on the Auburn. "What's up, buttercup?" she cooed.

Willie felt a shiver.

"Care to join me?" asked Loretta.

He had questions, and so, "Yes."

She popped the lock up on the passenger door.

Willie tugged it open. Slid inside and slammed it shut.

The car's upholstery smelled like Rico.

She turned the key in the ignition. "How 'bout we take a little ride."

"Sure," said Willie, having no clue where Loretta planned to take him. Or why she'd borrowed Rico's Auburn. *Had she followed him? She could have if she saw him board the Red Car, knowing the water taxis left from Seal Beach.*

He intended to find out. This didn't feel like a coincidence.

But something in his gut said to be careful.

Loretta wore a lowcut fuzzy sweater and big hoop earrings like she came here to meet sailors and to charge them for the privilege. Her faux-pearl necklace pendulated where cultured pearls did not belong. She shook a Marlboro from her pack of cigarettes atop the dashboard.

Willie squeezed the armrest on the door to calm his nerves.

She asked Willie for a light. Revved the engine, still in neutral.

He lit a match out of the matchbook he had borrowed from the *Tango* that was still inside his trouser pockets. Both his hands were trembling. He fumbled his way through it, nearly scorching his left thumb.

"Something wrong, Willie?" she asked. She signaled right onto Coast Highway, slipped the Auburn into first, exhaled smoke, and let the clutch out.

Willie stammered out the words, "What the hell happened to Rico?"

The car lurched forward with a jerk. Loretta swung out into traffic, looking over her left shoulder. She settled in behind a Buick and slowed down.

"He had an accident last week. The sort that doesn't make the news. You didn't hear?"

"Sure, I did." Willie sat up and faked a grin. He cocked his head like he expected that Loretta might be slightly more forthcoming, but she wasn't. "Swell how he didn't hurt his car."

"That was uncalled for," snapped Loretta.

Willie leaned back in his seat. He didn't trust her any more than he could throw her lying lips into San Pedro Bay offshore. *No way in hell,* he told himself,. She knew more than she let on, and she was good at playing dumb. But she was not who she appeared to be. She'd lied too many times, and Willie wondered what Loretta *really* knew about Enrico.

She puffed her cigarette and stared out through the windshield at the traffic. She drove southeast along Coast Highway. Tobacco smoke trailed from her fingers. A mile east of Seal Beach Boulevard, she pulled a full u-turn and settled in behind a bakery truck for Roman Meal Bread.

Willie thought she might be nervous or wasn't used to Rico's car. Every time she shifted gears, they groaned in agony and lurched. Her eyes kept darting back and forth the way dishonest people's eyes moved.

Willie wiped sweat from his forehead. "I kinda thought you'd be with Jack."

She took a long drag off her Marlboro. She wasn't saying much tonight. Willie sat motionless, hoping silence might encourage her to talk.

The outside air rustled her hair. Her fingers choked around the steering wheel, ten-o'clock and two, the way they taught you in the books. She seemed to compensate too much. It made him fear she'd had a drink or two. She tossed her head back, "I guess Jack and I had a minor – disagreement."

That was a start. He rolled his window down and stared out at the roadside. "That unusual?" asked Willie.

"He has a temper," said Loretta.

"That why he came to Santa Ana?"

"Will you stop the inquisition? It was a business trip," she said. "I didn't see him. I got lucky. Somehow I managed to avoid him."

"What sort of 'business' was Jack on?"

"It's complicated."

"Is it?"

Loretta stared out through the windshield and didn't say much more. She seemed a cypher, her lips extruded in a calculated pout. "Some things are better left alone, Willie."

He wondered about Jack, whether he'd poisoned old man Norton, why he'd gotten rid of Rico, if it tied in with Elena. *Too many deaths. Even a rape. Were they all somehow connected?* Willie's gut was whispering they were.

But then Loretta's lies made Willie wonder what he really knew. Might be convenient to pin all the blame on old Suicide Jack. But it seemed overly "convenient" how Loretta had the Auburn. At least for now. *Was she involved?* Something about it didn't smell right.

A traffic semaphore along Coast Highway rang out "STOP." He felt the brakes, and the car slowed.

"Why are you driving Rico's Auburn?"

Loretta snuffed her cigarette out.

"That was a question," Willie said.

Loretta shifted into neutral at the signal.

She didn't bat an eye. She rolled her window down and flicked her cigarette stub to the shoulder. She shook her hair out. Glanced at Willie. "I like driving it," she said.

"Well I guess Rico won't be needing it." Willie turned to face her.

She cocked her head and looked away.

The signal changed. The semaphore swung up for "GO."

Shifting the Auburn into gear, she slammed her foot down on the gas. Willie felt the car accelerate. She cruised along Coast Highway, speeding across the county line entering Long Beach city limits.

Glimmering lights from Naples Island shone off Alamitos Bay and the marina. They drove past Recreation Park up to the traffic circle.

"Where are we going?" Willie asked.

"Where do you want to go?" she said. She signaled right onto the traffic circle. Drove around the loop, following signs for State Route 1 and made a right turn at a stop sign. From there Coast Highway headed westward toward Long Beach and the harbor, past a score of residential streets that headed toward the beach.

Willie pointed at the dashboard. "Looks like we're gonna need some gas." It was on empty. There was a Hancock Station up by Cherry Avenue. She signaled right. Pulled to the pump. The station air hose didn't ring. Willie stepped out of the passenger seat and stomped down on the hose. Walked to the office. "Buy me some Marlboros," called Loretta, "and twelve gallons of ethyl."

The sleepy gas station attendant rang the sale in the office for a dollar forty-nine and followed Willie to the pumps. He kept gawking at the Auburn. Loretta's nails drummed the dashboard like she didn't want attention and had something on her mind. Willie handed her the cigarettes.

"Sweetie, put those in the glove box," she said.

Willie popped it open.

And he froze.

There was an ammo box, unopened, full of Colt 38 Supers, the sort of rounds he knew could penetrate a car door with no trouble. Usually cops had them, and gangsters. But Loretta was no gangster. *Or was she?*

He shut the glove compartment. Didn't say a word.

"You eat yet, Willie?"

"I'm not hungry."

"You're awfully quiet," said Loretta.

"I've been thinking."

"About what?"

"What do *you* think?" Willie fired back. "I feel like someone's out to get me. And I couldn't help but notice there were bullets…"

"Those were Rico's."

"Ah, but you know all about them. Where's the gun?" he asked Loretta.

She fired up the engine, and she didn't say a word. She let the clutch out. She hung a hard right onto Cherry and sped north toward Signal Hill. The smell of oil wells overpowered him. Raw air fanned Willie's face and burned his eyes. The Long Beach Harbor lights had disappeared from view. There was no moon. No stars. No streetlights.

He still wondered where the gun was.

There was her purse down in the floorwell in a place he couldn't reach it

A chilly fog from off the waters seemed to cling to Signal Hill. Atop the grade, she didn't signal but turned right on Skyline Drive, climbing the hill up past a reservoir, an empty city park, an open field.

Loretta pulled off from the road.

Turned the ignition off.

Rolled the windows shut.

Opened up her purse.

A gun fell out. Loretta grabbed it, a Colt 0. 38 Superautomatic.

She was shaking like an automatic paint mixer as she pointed it at Willie.

Willie's jaw dropped.

She gave a nod. "We need to talk."

CHAPTER XVI

SIGNAL HILL: MONDAY, APRIL 11

Willie's pulse raced like those freight trains screaming north to San Francisco, "Black Widow" engines hauling coal-black Southern Pacific Overnighters. Loretta'd tricked him. He never should have trusted her at all. She wasn't like Elena. Clearly poor Loretta had gone crazy. The gun was pointed right between his eyes.

She wanted something. That was obvious.

Willie wanted something, too. "Put the gun down, please," he muttered. "What on earth are you so scared of?"

Loretta shook her head.

Sweat beads poured from Willie's forehead. He breathed as shallowly as possible, afraid to even move.

Fog lifted off San Pedro Bay. Breezes rolled in from the shore, clearing the skies enough so Willie saw a dim light from the ocean four miles out. Might be the *Tango*, but right now it seemed more perilous right here, in Signal Hill.

The scent of oil wells soured the night.

"I don't feel safe without a pistol." The gun was wobbling in her hand. She sounded hoarse, like she'd been crying, but she hadn't shed a tear since he'd been with her. "I need protection."

"Doesn't Jack take care of that?"

Loretta smirked, then laughed out loud. "I can't believe you. God, that's rich."

"Someone informed me Jack killed Rico."

"You were *mis*informed," she said.

Cold air gusting from the harbor seemed to solidify Loretta. Her face froze like a sculpture made of ice. Her hair blew snake-like. Her stare could turn a man to stone. She glared at Willie in the moonlight.

Willie dared not turn away. Her eyes looked hard as steel ball bearings. She moved her pistol. Aimed it dead between his eyes and froze in place, holding it steady with both hands. She only had to pull the trigger. Willie's brief unhappy life flashed through his mind.

Loretta whispered, "I killed Rico."

Holy crap! Talk about crazy.

Willie pressed up against the car door. Fear was amplifying his senses. Foghorns moaned out from the ocean. He heard cars from Cherry Avenue. The breeze rustled the eucalyptus leaves somewhere outside. He heard her breathing. His pulse pounded machine-like through his temples. His heart hammered. The breeze felt like he'd walked into a freezer.

Holy Mary, mother of God! The way she'd said it, with no feeling, like a switch got flipped, and she'd become a sick cold-blooded killer. "You did.... What?"

"You don't know half of it." She said the sentence slowly.

Willie glanced down at his watch and breathed in deep.

This was waaay more than he'd bargained for, a good time to tread lightly. *Better not to show emotion. Let her talk and spill her guts.*

"*He* wanted *her* to take my place."

"*Who* wanted *who* to take your place?"

Loretta mouthed "Enrico." Her lips then formed the word "Elena." The barrel of her 0. 38 locked straight toward Willie's forehead. She didn't move.

Willie's gut wrenched inside-out. He dared not breathe.

"But she...." It all came into focus. Rico must have found Loretta "inconvenient," perhaps irrational, the way she was right now. Better to find a younger substitute who looked exactly like her. That way the cops would never need to open up that safe deposit box and find out what was in there because "Loretta" wasn't dead yet.

"You told me Rico was your business partner."

"*Was*. He was my handler. Let's use a blunter term. Enrico was my *pimp*. And all I wanted was Elena to find somebody like you and raise a family. Give me grandchildren, to live the life I longed for."

It was starting to make sense. But he was staring down the barrel of that Superautomatic with the rounds to blow his head off. He dared not make a move, not while Loretta was still talking.

"Only Enrico, he made *other* plans. He introduced Elena to my boyfriend, Jack, and brought her to Jack's cabin on the *Tango*. Elena calls me ship-to-shore. Says Jack raped her. Says Jack swears he's gonna kill *me*. And kill *you*. I suspect Jack killed *Elena*. I never told Jack how you slept with me, but somehow he found out, and he gets even in ways only Jack can do."

That greedy tattooed horny bastard. Willie longed to throttle Jack. *Man ruined everything he touched, José's friendship. Elena's sweetness. Elena's love. Willie's good name. Even Loretta's lousy life*. Willie had wondered why Loretta'd set him up inside her bungalow, invited *him* into her bedroom.

Now he knew.

He fought to mask his rage. *Keep your yap shut,* Willie told himself. *At some point, she'll calm down.* He thought of grabbing for her gun or maybe knocking it away. *Far too dangerous,* he thought. Plus, he was backed against the car door where he couldn't reach the gun. Jump from the car. *But there was only one road out. She had the car keys. Plus, the gun. It was dicey.*

Nobody could outrun bullets.

Loretta's hand no longer trembled. She held that gun like it was locked into a vise and aimed straight at him.

"What do you want from me?" he asked.

"An escort. My *own* escort." Loretta reached to grab a smoke but balked at laying down her pistol. She set her jaw and tossed her unlit cigarette onto the floormat.

"And what precisely do you want with your own escort?" Willie asked.

"You drive me back to Seal Beach."

"I can do that," Willie said.

"You're making sense now. To Vivian Laird's Garden of Allah where I show you a good time." Loretta winked, a practiced motion she had mastered.

"Swell. I can jitterbug at gunpoint. What a hoot." Willie replied.

"What? Don't you like me?"

She held that pistol, and her question wasn't hard. There were two choices. One was, "Of course, I like you." The other choice was dying.

"Of course, I like you," Willie muttered. Best to choose the safer option.

"We need each other," said Loretta. "Otherwise Jack's gonna kill you since you slept with me and know he screwed you over with his Charlie Boards. He murdered Norton just to set you up so cops would haul you in. Except so far, they haven't found you. Jack can be a bit impatient, not being a citizen and coming from Straits Settlements, from Singapore. It's why he lives outside of U. S. jurisdiction."

"On the *Tango*."

"Cops can't touch him, but he can't file a complaint if he gets cross."

"Might be easier if you and I split town."

"And leave Elena unavenged?"

"Well, it beats suicide," said Willie. "And it's not like we can resurrect Elena."

Loretta's face turned cold. "I didn't know you were a coward, Willie. Elena truly loved you. She was *raped* by Suicide Jack. He'll keep on raping if you let him. Other girls are gonna die. The cops can't stop the man."

"Unless...."

Loretta gazed into his eyes. "Unless," she whispered. She lowered one hand from her gun and touched his wrist.

"Unless we *do* something," said Willie, setting his jaw against the night. Willie shivered. Loretta needed him. He also needed *her*. He longed for justice, something the law in California wasn't offering to people like himself, or like Loretta, or Elena. And since Jack wasn't a citizen, Willie only knew one way.

He nodded, knowing they'd need to take the law into their hands. He wasn't wild for vigilantes, but the law left them no choice.

"Okay, I'm in," he told Loretta.

She put the gun back in her purse.

Gave him the car keys.

Willie swallowed.

Stepping outside, they swapped seats.

Willie fired up the Auburn, slipped the engine into gear, and drove the car to Seal Beach in total silence.

The Spanish arches and Moorish towers at Vivian Laird's Garden of Allah glowed pale orange beneath the moonlight from the neon sign above. Cars were parked along Coast Highway. Willie found an empty space two blocks away on Central Avenue, a quarter mile from Eighth Street. He raised the roof on the convertible. He locked up all the doors. Loretta told him they would need to leave the car for several days.

Outside, Loretta clutched his hand like they were going on a date. She had her purse tucked in the other hand and strapped around her shoulder. A sailor whistled at her. Willie didn't turn his head. They walked together in the moonlight toward the arches and the tower up ahead, where evidently there were still remaining tickets.

Beneath a row of missing lightbulbs on a dirty tiled wall he saw a sailor stop to urinate. The piss stench turned his nose. Disgusted, Willie picked their pace up, walking briskly toward the sizzling neon signage shining above Vivian Laird's Garden of Allah.

Loretta walked next to his shoulder. It was a side of her that Willie'd never seen. Like she was proud to be his date. Proud to be seen with him. It lifted Willie's spirits. It felt good to be admired. He only wished it was Elena, but he didn't dare to say it.

Two tickets, including chicken or steak dinners, cost eight dollars. Loretta opened up her purse and paid the uniformed cashier. People inside had finished eating. They were bringing out desserts and serving cocktails. Loretta ushered him inside.

He had his doubts about tonight. Up front, Jack Teagarden was playing his trombone, *After You've Gone*, the Bessie Smith song from the Twenties. Loretta asked Willie to dance, and he agreed to just one number. She tugged him out onto the dance floor, pulled him close. She cooed the lyrics just like Bessie used to sing them back before Willie was born.

After you've gone and left me cryin',

After you've gone there's no denyin',

You're gonna feel blue, and you're gonna feel sad,

...You'll miss the bestest pal you ever had.

She felt warm inside his arms. He overlooked that she had been Elena's mother and imagined she was actually Elena. He'd forgotten how it felt to hold a woman in his arms, but he enjoyed it now. A man needed bright moments in his life. Sometimes you took whatever pleasures life served up.

Her earrings sparkled. Bluesy notes poured from Jack Teagarden's trombone. *Body and Soul.* Willie drew close to her. She wrapped her languid arms around his back like they were both in a cocoon, cozy and warm, just like two monarchs on a milkweed, on a balmy summer day before they fly away to Mexico where predators won't hurt them.

Sailors and girls slid to the edges of the dance floor when the song ended. Jack Teagarden segued into *Frenesí* on the trombone. Loretta pulled Willie against her. She shut her eyes like she remembered what was playing on the Sears Silvertone radio one night back at her Santa Ana bungalow. And Willie danced along, wondering what Loretta thought, wondering what he thought himself. She seemed to smile like she knew something he didn't as they danced.

They heard loud popping. Loretta grabbed him by his wrist. They rushed outside to see the "Fountains of Flame" fireworks being launched up from the pier. Sparks filled the sky with reds and oranges. Willie smelled the smoke and sulfur, heard the ooohs, the ahhs, the sizzles, and fire crackling from the sky, a grand finale. Loretta smiled like a schoolgirl as if this were the first time she'd seen fireworks. Their glow lit up Loretta's face, and it was almost like a curtain had been pulled back to reveal another side of her, not the tough and hard-shell woman he was used to. Rather a girl who now recalled some better angels from her childhood.

And then the skies went dark, excepting for the pale crescent moon, some stars, and ghostly shadows from the trusses near the Joy Zone and the roller coaster. High atop the scaffolding, the antiquated coaster cars were locked and braked in place up high where hobos couldn't reach them. As Willie ambled toward the pier, he didn't hold Loretta's hand, like they'd been married many years, and life had settled down to business. The night felt chilly. Loretta led him up a dirty wooden staircase to a room she evidently had a key to.

She unlocked it.

The light was already left on. It was a studio apartment full of dust and mismatched pillows, and no dishes in the kitchen. Exhausted, Willie plopped down on the sofa to conk out. Tomorrow morning, they would ride the water taxi to the *Tango*.

They would confront Suicide Jack. Willie would need to get some sleep. He heard Loretta's preparations from her bedroom. He longed for rest, but he was nervous, and his stomach was in knots. He wondered if Elena even cared what he was doing, but he knew he had to vindicate her honor.

He shut his eyes, afraid to sleep but too worn out to stay awake. Footsteps padded toward him from the bedroom.

A soft kiss on his forehead.

A whisper.

"See you soon, baboon."

Willie winced. He took a breath, not expecting what he smelled. A second breath. He reconfirmed Loretta's breath was laced with vomit.

He winced.

It was hard to get to sleep.

CHAPTER XVII

SEAL BEACH: TUESDAY, APRIL 12

By moonlight Willie climbed the ladder up the roller coaster scaffolds. He'd been thinking that Elena was just 20 feet below him. He glanced down and saw Loretta. Next time he looked, no one was there. He was halfway to the top, and there were seagulls all around him. Atop the rotting wooden frame were weathered cars, locked in position near the crest where hobos couldn't scrawl graffiti on the shells. He hoped to sit up there and think, figure out where he was going. His life had come unraveled. Willie needed to make choices.

As he scrambled up the ladder, the lights of Seal Beach receded, reminding Willie of Lionel train sets in department stores at Christmas. He paused and shivered, his face buffeted by cold Pacific gusts that moaned and whistled past his ears and whipped damp hair across his forehead. His cheeks fluttered. The scaffold groaned. He hung on for dear life and muscled higher up the ladder. Salty mist burned in his eyes. His forearms throbbed, but he kept climbing.

Higher.

Higher.

Almost there.

He vaulted into the first car. The seat was spattered with white residue from shorebirds.

It appeared the gusts had settled.

He grabbed the rusty steel bar that was supposed to hold him in. It had corroded in position. Willie couldn't pull it down. Maybe a blessing, Willie thought. It allowed him to crawl out.

It surprised him the bird residue had vanished.

Surf crashed far beneath him. The stars were hard to see. The streets of Seal Beach were silent, no revelers, no drunken couples, no crowds outside of the Beach Theater, no sailors lined up at casinos. It must be late, *he thought. The seagulls had gone silent.*

But he felt wide awake and had a chance to think.

About Loretta. He didn't trust her.

About how Jack was out to kill him in a fight he didn't want. He had no choice but to fight back.

Then he'd do what?

The only thing he'd ever wanted was respect. But it was evident respect was hard to come by.

A cold gust shook the scaffold. Willie feared it might blow over. Stars were swaying overhead, and Willie clutched the steel bar to keep from falling, fearing the wind might lift the car up off the tracks and end it all.

What was the deal with Loretta?

She had seduced him. He regretted it so much the thought revolted him. He'd let her do it. Sometimes he sensed Loretta wanted him. But she had none of the sweetness he'd admired in

Elena. Loretta's soul had been scarred over. She'd loved Elena, tried to give the girl the things Loretta longed for, but for all Loretta's sacrifices, nothing had worked out. He felt pity for Loretta but couldn't say so. And yet somehow she controlled him. Why? *He wondered.*

Far offshore, Willie thought he saw the bright lights of the Tango. Today he'd go there with Loretta to avenge Elena's murder. It wasn't something he liked doing, but there were such things as honor. A man had obligations to fight for people whom he loved. He'd loved *Elena.*

He looked up and thought he saw Elena's face.

She wiped a tear out of her eye. "No vale la pena." *Elena whispered. "Please don't go. It isn't worth it."*

Her silken hair flowed in the breeze. He smelled those roses she had crushed behind her ears, and she was smiling just the way Willie remembered. He reached for her, to hold, to kiss, to hear her voice, to love. But she receded.

The roller coaster began moving.

As if the brakes had come undone, he careened downhill on a clacking bumpy track into a dip then made his way up a steep grade, a sharp quick turn. Salt spray from the ocean stung his cheeks. Willie was pressed against the car wall. Steel wheels groaned, the rails rattled, the scaffold moaned in unison. The stars swirled overhead. A sudden turn. A rise. A dip.

He coasted to a stop.

He stepped outside onto a boardwalk. Half the boards were missing. Willie walked toward a beach of cold dark sand that chilled his toes. There was Elena, her image drifting out to sea, but there were parrots all around her like he'd heard about in Mexico, and monarch butterflies ascended from the water.

There was a nudge on Willie's shoulder.

"Wake up, buttercup." It was Loretta.

He looked up at her.

She offered him a steaming cup of coffee. She grinned. She had her suitcase packed inside of her apartment.

Willie looked down at his watch. Six-thirty.

The boat left from the pier in twenty minutes.

Willie pulled his pants and shirt on. Shoved his shoes onto his feet. His heart raced, but he told himself he didn't have a choice. The taxi left in fifteen minutes. José had an expression. "Gotta be all in or all out. No such thing as halfway pregnant."

Willie'd promised he would help Loretta take down Suicide Jack. She handed him her suitcase. He opened up the door and made his way down wooden steps. Loretta locked the door behind them. She caught up to his side and started talking.

"So, here's the plan, orangutan, When I'm working on the *Tango*, Jack helps oversee the crap tables."

Willie made his way down Main Street toward the pier.

"Don't let him see you," said Loretta. "Stay on the deck. I settle in and do my job, flirting with customers, bringing drinks and cigarettes. After an hour, you come find us at the tables."

"Okay, so what do I do then?" Willie's nerves were still on edge.

"You don't let Jack out of your sight. He's stabbed at least a dozen people. In the back."

"Quite the professional."

"He survives," Loretta said. "The way a shark does." Her eyes narrowed, like she was holding something back. They reached the pier. The surf came pounding through the pilings.

Loretta's words were little comfort. Willie had seen Jack's muscled forearms, hands strong enough to crush a brick. He feared Loretta meant to set him up.

"I'll lay odds Suicide Jack will pick a fight," Loretta said. "It's how he operates. Just in case...." She touched her purse, reminding Willie she was carrying the gun.

He did *not* feel reassured.

He was unarmed. He didn't stand a bloody chance. He'd beat up Norton pretty bad, but that was different. Norton fought back fair and square. Willie expected Suicide Jack might would have a knife handy, or worse. It wasn't Willie's type of fighting, but he'd do it for Elena. And after that....

Loretta handed him his ticket.

"There's our taxi."

Willie felt as if he'd just swallowed a switchblade.

They made their way onto the boat. Willie found himself a seat cushion and life jacket. Loretta didn't sit beside him for the ride. "Best we not be seen together." She found a place up near the bow next to a pair of zozzled ladies. Willie moved toward the stern.

They left the dock. The boat chugged south toward a flock of circling pelicans. Its captain pointed out the place where Cecil B. DeMille had filmed the Red Sea being parted for the film, *The Ten Commandments*. A trio of tourists in Hawaiian shirts with Kodak Brownie cameras snapped flash photos of the beach, leaving spots in Willie's eyes. Then Willie noticed something odd, the roller coaster on the scaffolds on the beach had rolled downhill during the night.

He felt a shiver. The cars were resting where he'd seen them in his dream. But it had clearly been a dream, perhaps some sort of precognition. He wasn't sure what had occurred, perhaps there'd been some strange connection, an angel or free spirit had released the coaster's brakes while he'd been dreaming. Then Willie looked across the boat and felt his heart stop.

There was a copy of *The Santa Ana Register* a passenger was reading on the boat. Willie stared at the front page. It might as well have been his photograph, a drawing of himself from a police sketch of "The man accused of murdering Lawrence Norton".

Cold sweat formed on Willie's brow.

The water taxi chugged to sea. His heart was crawling up his throat. The pier receded behind the stern. The seas offshore were rough and choppy. Willie's stomach began twisting like he'd turned it upside-down.

He wanted off of this boat. Now.

He looked exactly like that drawing, but so far no one had noticed. And in an hour he'd be meeting up with Jack.

CHAPTER XVIII

ABOARD THE *S. S. TANGO*, TUESDAY, APRIL 12

Willie felt seasick. The boat ride to the *Tango* had been rough but seeing his image on the front page of the *Register* had been rougher. What the hell would he do now? Willie didn't have a clue. It was like GAME OVER in pinball, and he'd run out of spare change after he'd bought himself ten chips from the cashier.

From the deck he stared to sea just outside of the casino, making sure to face the shore, escaping notice. He was waiting for Loretta to settle in. He checked his watch. Nine-fifteen. An hour had elapsed since they had boarded.

His stomach twisted, and beads of perspiration soaked his brow. Jack was stronger than him, probably more ruthless. Willie straightened himself up and made his way toward the casino. His heart was hammering. He wished Suicide Jack wasn't aboard.

He entered the casino. Double leather-covered doors swung shut behind him. Slot machines jangled around him, bells and lights, spinning roulette wheels, green felt tables, stacks of poker chips, and taller stacks of playing cards. Foul smoke from cigarettes and stale cheap cigars poured through the the gaming room. A jackpot rang. The noise made Willie's head ache.

The smoke was thick enough to stir, so strong it watered Willie's eyes. He scanned the room. A sea of faces, murmurs, people crowding tables. None were smiling. Cigarette girls in high heels and fish-net stockings crossed the room bearing their merchandise. He glanced past the roulette tables.

There was Loretta.

Willie set his jaw and kept on walking.

She wore a lowcut orange blouse, showing off more flesh than it should above a skirt that made its way above her knees. She didn't smile. Their eyes met for a fraction of a second. She looked away.

Suicide Jack stood at the crap table, the stickman, wearing a diamond-studded shirt rolled up exposing his tattooed and muscled forearms. Biceps the size of Willie's head made Willie pause to reconsider. He shut his eyes.

He had to do this for Elena.

Willie walked past leather stools where women chatted and sipped cocktails whose little pink umbrellas impaled maraschino cherries. Beyond, fat men in baggy suits with short cigars nursed shots of bourbon. Four were standing at the crap table. A bottle blonde between them sported bingo wings as droopy as her out-of-fashion hat.

A spot was open. Willie edged up to the table with ten chips. The ditzy bottle blonde was rolling. Someone said her name was Doris. Willie placed his chips on PASS. She picked two dice, exhaled smoke on them and shook them hard enough to flap her wings.

The dice bounced off the backboard.

"Yo-leven," Jack called out. That high-pitched voice again. So jarring.

Willie exhaled. He grinned wide. Doris had just doubled his money. Jack was looking his direction. "So loverboy here just got lucky." He fired a side glance at Loretta, then he zeroed in on Willie. "Let's try again, champ. Double or nothin." Part of Jack's lip tilted up slightly.

Willie swallowed back his nerves. He bet on PASS and set his jaw. Hot perspiration soaked the backside of his ears.

The dice were moved to an Italian in a brown-feathered fedora. He rolled the dice with a quick sweep.

Jack called out, "Nina from Catalina."

It was a nine, and Willie's 20 chips remained out on the table. The Italian rolled again, while Willie sucked in both his cheeks.

"Little Joe from Kokomo."

Fedora man had rolled a four. He shut his eyes and exhaled smoke onto the dice.

He shook again.

Suicide Jack glared at Loretta, a glance so cold it should have snuffed her cigarette out. Loretta looked down at her tray and slid from view.

Willie glanced down at his tokens.

Fedora man tossed both the dice. They shot like bullets across the table and recoiled against the backboard.

"Nina from Pasadena," came the call from Suicide Jack.

Momentary joy filled Willie's veins.

He took a breath, but he knew better than to smile when he won.

The boxman doubled Willie's chips, giving him forty.

Willie hoped old lady luck was on his side, not for the chips but for the battle he was hoping to avoid.

He slid his chips back to the PASS line. A pair of men had left the table. It was Willie's turn to roll. Suicide Jack passed him the dice. Willie thought he saw a smirk.

"Feelin' lucky, loverboy?"

He didn't even want to be here. He'd had a modest streak of luck, but he was thinking about how he would approach Suicide Jack. Loretta didn't have a plan, only a gun inside her purse, and somehow Willie was supposed to win a fight with Suicide Jack.

Willie didn't say a word. The dice felt cold. He chose two others, rubbed them both against his shirt to warm them up and squeezed them hard.

Loretta stood a step behind Jack. Both her hands covered her purse, her face expressionless and chilly as the ocean.

Willie wiped sweat from off his brow onto his sleeve. He breathed in deep, studied the cubes in his right hand. They were green, with little emblems of the *Tango* on each die. Willie blew on them for luck and shook them hard in his right fist.

He let them go.

Both of them bounced against the backboard.

Double fives.

"Hard ten, a lady's little friend." Jack looked straight at Willie. At Loretta. His small lips flatlined. But behand Jack's sea-gray eyes, Willie sensed rage was boiling over. Willie hadn't missed the irony despite Jack's blank expression.

All of Willie's chips were on the table and at risk.

Willie blew against the dice.

Let them go.

"Hard ten again."

More chips were pushed Willie's direction.

A crowd had gathered at the crap table.

Willie gathered up his winnings, eighty chips piled up in front of him, and everyone was watching.

Suicide Jack massaged his forearm with his gaze glued to Loretta.

Her cigarette was moving in slow-motion.

"You know this stranger?" Jack pointed his stick Willie's direction. It was clear what he was asking.

"Never seen him," said Loretta.

"Fat chance, old gal," Jack muttered back. Clearly, he knew Loretta'd lied. He glared at Willie. "Put your money down or get off my damn table.

Jack laid ten chips down.

"I said *all* of it."

Willie shook his head.

Jack whipped his stick at Willie's face, smack on the nose. It snapped in half.

A stab of pain. Willie reached up. Blood was squirting out both nostrils. Fear flickered through him.

Jack came strolling his direction, both fists clenched. "Think I don't know a few things, *cholo?* You think ol' Jack don't know what time it is? It's payback time," he bellowed. Jack threw a punch.

Willie ducked under it.

Jack fought to regain balance. Propped himself against the crap table. Spit his snuff wad into Willie's startled face.

The crowd moved back.

Willie heard murmurs, He wiped spittle from his forehead and flung it down onto the floor. His stomach flinched, he gagged, looked up, and gulped for air.

Bouncers moved forward, but Loretta stared them down and said to both, "Stay out of this."

Willie looked up, and so did Jack.

A man was standing in the corner in a hat. It was "The Admiral."

"Tony Cornero," someone whispered.

Tony stood there like a man who owned both stallions in a horse race. He fired a grin at both the bouncers. "You heard the lady," Tony said. The Admiral gave a nod, and people slowly edged aside. "Looks like we got an altercation. Two-to-one odds on my stickman. Five-to-two odds on the spic-man. Boxman here'll take your bets."

Suicide Jack lifted up Willie and threw him hard against the table.

Willie staggered to his feet, feeling cold rage surge inside him. Warm blood seeped across his lip leaving a harsh metallic taste that soured his tongue. Willie glared at Jack. He'd never felt such fury. Everything was piling up, the hatred he'd endured from Mildred, Stanley, Norton, common people, the dirty tricks, Elena's *rape*. His fury seemed to double strength as if he'd tapped into the spirit of his ancestors, from Ireland, his mother's tribe, the Yaquis from Sonora.

Willie lowered his head, and like a *toro* he charged Jack.

They collided on the carpet. A champagne glass crunched beneath them. They threw punches at each other. Willie connected with a jab against Jack's nose. "That's for José after you cleaned out all his Charlie Boards." Another punch. "For poisoning Norton."

Blood was seeping from Jack's gums.

Jack spit again, and Willie recoiled but recovered his composure. He wiped Jack's blood from off his jaw. Flung it back into Jack's face. Jack was beneath him and within Willie's control. Eyeball-to-eyeball, Willie murmured, "Who *raped* Elena Valenzuela?"

The truth was all over Jack's face which had gone redder than a stop sign.

"Who *killed* Elena Valenzuela?"

Jack lay silent.

Willie knew. A head of steam boiled inside him, and his temples banged like pistons below deck.

Jack's gaze darted, his eyes the size of silver dollars. Then he shrugged. He clearly hadn't mastered lying. Willie hammered Jack's stunned face. Again. Again. A blaze of rage, and gore came gushing out Jack's nose. Jack shut his eyes and blood came dripping from one lid.

Then he lay still.

"I ought to kill you," Willie whispered.

High heels click-click-clacked behind him, and Loretta grabbed his fist. She pressed her gun into his grip.

She stepped away.

He felt a shudder.

"Do it," said Loretta.

Loretta's gun felt like an ice block.

"Kill him."

Willie hesitated.

"Pull the goddamn trigger. For Elena. KILL HIM. NOW!"

The crowd was chanting with her. "Kill-kill-kill."

Willie couldn't pull the trigger. He was shaking.

A snap of metal.

Steel plunged into his thigh. Pain ricocheted through Willie's leg. He felt the cold twist of a switchblade.

Closed his eyes to block out anguish.

Jack exploded back to life smashing a chop to Willie's forearm, knocking the gun from Willie's fist. The arm went limp. A bone lump throbbed above the wrist. *Probably broken.* Loretta's gun slid out of reach across the deck. One of the bouncers picked it up.

A surging Jack tossed Willie up and rolled across him.

Willie's wrist pounded with agony.

Jack was now on top of Willie with the knife raised up and looking like some ancient Aztec warrior readied up for human sacrifice. He stroked its steel past Willie's throat. Willie's forearm throbbed. Jack's bleeding face glared down at Willie, livid red and demonlike, and forces Willie didn't understand swelled up inside him.

Willie squirmed and wiggled free. Enough to bite into Jack's wrist.

A howl.

The knife dropped.

Loretta grabbed it from the deck and slipped aside.

Willie rolled on top of Jack, slamming Jack's skull against the deck, bashing it down, ramming the elbow just above his aching wrist onto Jack's throat. Hurt like a banshee. Willie swallowed back the pain and fought to live.

Jack's head snapped back. He gasped for air.

Willie pressed harder. Bit back pain.

A feeble squirm.

Another smash from Willie's elbow crushed Jack's larynx like a mailing tube.

Jack fought to gulp in air. His crushed throat whistled with each breath.

His eyes bulged larger than fresh eggs.

Then he lay still.

"Kill him," Loretta snapped her fingers, tapped her heel on the deck.

"I can't." said Willie, who looked up at her in terror. His insides froze.

"Kill the man, you goddamn coward."

Willie trembled and shook harder.

Loretta cursed a bloody streak. Bent down a foot above Jack's face.

Mashed the switchblade through Jack's eye like that tattoo on Jack's right forearm.

Willie cringed. He looked away and choked back vomit.

Squirts of blood oozed up in spurts around the blade and down Jack's cheek. There was a moan. Jack's body quivered in slow motion as the blood drained.

Like a battery running low, Jack's pulse was slowing.

Willie leaned against Jack's chest, felt him bleed out until, at last, the man lay still.

There was silence for a minute and a half.

Willie's heart thrummed like a kettledrum. He had yet to catch his breath. His head was swimming with emotion. One deep gasp. He held it in.

And then the room came into focus, and the crowds surrounded all of them, and lines formed at a crap table where Tony's men were paying off the wagers. The engines started below deck, making the switchblade handle wiggle over Jack's eye like those speed bags at the gym.

It finally stopped.

Willie exhaled.

Loretta frowned at Willie. "Throw this worthless bastard overboard," she told him with contempt.

He didn't care to, but he hoisted up the corpse with his good arm and somehow balanced it. Flipped the mass across his bruised and battered shoulder. Staggered past empty green felt tables, stumbled outside through double doors from the casino to the deck and to the railings on the gunwale. With a heave he rolled the corpse into the cold Pacific waters.

A splash. A bloody pool encircled Jack. The sun was glaring off the ocean.

Willie could breathe now. His pulse was slowing back to normal.

The body floated on the surface. Blood swirled and pinwheeled through the waters. Willie watched. He didn't like being a killer. Not one bit. All he had wanted was Elena.

Someone was muttering behind him. "Don't be pissin' off no *cholos*."

Someone laughed.

Willie spun and looked around.

The laughing stopped.

Disgusted, Willie walked away. He saw his watch. He didn't need a souvenir, nor did he want one anymore. He slipped the watch off from his swollen arm and thrust it toward Loretta. Said, "I think this might be yours."

He couldn't even bear to look at her.

Loretta slid the watch onto her arm.

She lit a cigarette.

Blood soaked both of Willie's battered hands. He wiped it off onto his trousers. Loretta'd shown him how to kill a man, a skill he didn't want. Blood ran inside of him like icewater. *Sangfroid,* like the French said. He stared toward Catalina, toward Jack's bobbing mass of flesh, Jack's studded shirt, the mop of hair, the bloody crater where Loretta'd jammed Jack's knife into his brain. At least the knife had fallen out.

Loretta stood at Willie's side, shaking her head at Suicide Jack. She puffed her Marlboro. Smoke rose up from its tip in errant tendrils. She let her cigarette burn down until it almost seared her fingernails. Frowned. Took one last puff and eyed its smoldering orange tip. A wispy parachute of smoke swirled overhead.

"Blow a kiss, jellyfish," muttered Loretta with a smirk. She tossed her cigarette toward Jack into the water.

She laughed out loud and lit another.

Willie backed away.

"What's wrong?" Loretta asked.

Willie swallowed back revulsion.

"You know the law doesn't apply out here. We're outside U. S. waters," said Loretta.

He shut his eyes. He wished he'd never known this woman. Elena had been sweet. It seemed Loretta had been ruined, filled with rage and cigarette smoke and an ice block for a heart.

Willie feared the same was happening to him.

"You should stop smoking," Willie said. "Those nasty cigarettes'll kill you."

Loretta snorted. She took a long drag off her Marlboro and frowned.

She exhaled in Willie's face and turned away. Took one last gander at Jack's corpse.

Then she strolled without a word into the sun. Her high heels slapped against the deck. Her footsteps paused. She spun around. Loretta's silhouette was waving. Willie heard her blow a kiss.

"Toodle-oo, kangaroo."

She turned around and kept on walking.

Her footsteps faded, replaced by seagulls making naughty little noises overhead like they were telling dirty jokes.

CHAPTER XIX

ABOARD THE *S. S. TANGO*, WEDNESDAY, APRIL 13

Willie felt chilly. Loretta had just walked out of his life, and he had no clue where she'd gone. But he had problems of his own. Both of Tony Cornero's bouncers slowly sauntered his direction. Tony'd just lost a good stickman. Willie feared that had upset him. He also worried Tony'd lost a bit of money on the wagers.

The bouncers muscled up to Willie. "Boss says you need to go ashore."

Willie said nothing. He was still trying to fathom what had happened.

The other bouncer stood on deck, reading *The Santa Ana Register.* He looked at Willie." Somethin's familiar. Don't I know youse from somewhere?"

And then he smiled like the lights had been switched on inside his brain. The bouncer tapped against his newspaper.

"Yeah, I thought youse looked familiar. The sorts I meets on ocean cruises never ceases to amaze me."

His partner jammed Loretta's gun in Willie's throat. "You're comin' with us."

Willie's heart returned to overdrive. He tensed. "And going where?"

"Seal Beach. We'll have 'em send a special water taxi, boy."

"Bullfrog," said Willie. "Nope, I ain't goin' back on land." He shook his head. "I get a phone call. Ship-to-shore."

"You'll make that call from Santa Ana."

"No sirs," Willie deadpanned. "'Cause I don't think you want me spilling beans to the police. My girlfriend died out here. Elena Valenzuela. She was raped. Her father, Javy Valenzuela also died aboard the *Tango*. It would be very bad for business if my people learned the truth."

Bluffing, Willie did his best to keep his face straight.

There was a pause. Willie was pretty sure the bouncers he addressed knew all about how Javy'd won his bet and wound up going overboard. Perhaps they'd done the deed themselves. The way they spoke backed up his hunch. Maybe they'd do the same to Willie. It was happening a lot.

"Javy was murdered," Willie said. He lowered his voice." Loretta told me." He did his best to keep a poker face.

The bouncers didn't flinch.

The bouncers had a conversation outside Willie's earshot. Tony Cornero came and said something. His fist pounded his palm, and then he nodded.

Willie found himself escorted by both bouncers to a small room near the bow end of the Tango.

Inside, a woman in a print dress full of poinciana flowers manned a radio. "Who we callin'?"

Willie gave her Stanley's number.

He wasn't sure Stanley was home. He had his doubts Stanley was sober. He got Mildred on the telephone.

"I need to talk to Stanley."

"This sounds like Willie. Stanley's gone."

"Will he be back?"

"He was evicted. Try the tavern. Tell him I said to go to hell."

Willie frowned, thinking of words even Loretta never used. "You got a number for Hub's Tavern?"

"Look it up."

"I'm on a ship."

"Yeah, right," she said.

Angry, Willie drummed the handset with his fingers.

A foghorn blew.

"By Jupiter, you are, Willie," said Mildred. She seemed surprised. Her manner changed to sweet-enough-to-make-your-ears-bleed.

Moments later, Mildred gave Willie the number to write down. "And don't forget to tell that lush where he can stick it like you promised."

"Thanks," said Willie.

He wrote the number on his hand.

It surprised Willie that Stanley even picked up the bar's phone. "Right, this is Stan." He sounded zozzled. "Da hell you want witch me."

"It's Willie."

"What?"

"I said it's Willie. Used to live with you. Garage in Santa Ana. Got your number from that harpy you shacked up with. Mildred says she tossed you out. Kinda surprised she even spoke with me.

"Lousy bitch."

"Stan, I'm in trouble."

"That ol' hag treated you like dirt. It wasn't right."

"I know," said Willie. "But I need help." He drummed the phone. Stan was all talk. He'd never helped Willie before.

Willie bit his lip and said a prayer.

Stanley gave a little snort. "Askin' Mildred for a favor's kinda like askin' Smith and Wesson to do surgery," he bellowed.

"I didn't ask her. I asked *you*."

There was a pause. Both Tony's bouncers kept on looking at the radio. At Willie. At the radio. One tapped his shoe against the deck.

The lady in the print dress said, "The call is still in progress."

"Wrap it up," muttered a bouncer.

Stanley kept talking. Said, "I'm sorry. I'm a drunk."

"Sir, I need help, not a confession," Willie said and then told Stanley what had happened on the *Tango*.

Stanley listened. He interrupted just enough so Willie knew he was still there, the way he'd never been before, except he was there.

"I know exactly what to do, son."

Willie had never heard those words. They sent a shiver up his spine.

"I know this guy. From in my Navy days. Recruiter."

Willie straightened. "Whoa, I don't wanna join no Navy."

"Hell yeah, you do. You got no choice."

Willie looked around. Both bouncers stared in his direction. Both were witnesses to Suicide Jack's murder. He'd helped do it. Not to mention Norton's death for which he'd probably get blamed.

The stocky bouncer drummed the countertop. He seemed to be impatient.

"I'll call the Coast Guard," Stanley said. "These guys got ways of workin' out stuff. I'm suggestin' you enlist."

"But?"

"Kid, I love you, but any Mexican is screwed, blued, and tattooed in California. Your mother swore the deck was stacked when the Americans deported her and bussed her into Mexico."

"Say what?" said Willie, stunned.

"July sixth, nineteen-thirty-one. I loved that gal."

Willie stood spellbound. He'd never heard a word of *this*.

Stanley wept as he told Willie what had happened to his mother on a hot day in July. "I'd just come home from welding car frames at Pacific Electric's car barns. And Maria wasn't home. I waited up for her till midnight.

"Next day Maria's still not home. So, I goes down to the police station. Get stonewalled. Lousy cops tell me it happens all the time.

"Two weeks later I get this postcard all the way from Hermosillo. Maria's beggin' me to mail her twenty bucks. Writes me they won't let her come home. Says they'll arrest her if she sets foot in California."

Willie'd heard stories about busses being filled up full of "Mexicans," a lot of whom were born in California, and bussed "home". Most of their parents had come north during the Mexican Revolution, or Cristero Wars, or had been here when the land was part of Mexico. People born in California had been shipped across the border when Midwesterners showed up in California needing jobs. The thought had not crossed Willie's mind they might have bussed away his *mother*. Stanley had never said a word. Only now it all made sense, his mother's disappearance, Stanley turning alcoholic, the loneliness Willie'd endured. *What might have happened if his mother could have stayed? God only knew.*

He wiped his eyes.

Stuff like this should have been illegal.

"I'll call the Coast Guard, son. God bless you," Stanley said and hung the phone up.

Willie slammed the phone down.

He wasn't sure how to react.

Stanley was drunk, and Willie wasn't sure the Coast Guard would show up. He found a bench across the radio room. Sat down, propping his head between his hands, swallowing tears, telling himself he'd never drink the way poor Stanley had. He'd prove that Irish-Mexicans were *strong*. He wiped his face clean. No time to grieve knowing the white people were watching.

He'd be a stoic. He was used to it, had practiced it. Perfected it.

A bouncer placed a hand on Willie's shoulder.

From the horizon came a light. Its beam reflected off the ocean, a Coast Guard cutter, white and gray with stark black letters on the hull. When it arrived, three men in uniform found Willie and the bouncers by the gangway where the water taxis came to pick up passengers.

They escorted him on board. And motored south.

Willie stared out toward the ocean and a massive bed of kelp off to his left. To his right, the silhouette of Catalina. The seas were choppy, but the motion didn't bother him today. Perhaps he'd finally found his sealegs. He'd been told that he would need them. A flying fish jumped from the water, sailed a foot above the surface, disappeared beneath the sea five seconds later.

"Where are we going?" Willie asked.

"San Diego," came the answer. "Naval Training Center. Boot Camp. You take your physical tomorrow. You're gonna be there seven weeks, boy. Can you swim?"

Willie said, "Yes."

"That's a good thing," said a man who was reportedly an ensign. "The Navy likes recruits if they can swim."

"I'm a *good* swimmer," said Willie.

The man walked off. "I'm sure you are."

Willie stared out past the stern. The Coast Guard cutter rocked beneath him. He could feel the vibrations of the engine through his shoes. The sun stood high at twelve o'clock. There were no shadows on deck.

The Long Beach shoreline and the *Tango* had receded out of view.

Willie felt nervous, but he was good at looking brave.

CHAPTER XX

SANTA ANA: SATURDAY, SEPTEMBER 16, 1944

Behind the Culligan water softener in Loretta's new back yard the transplant bathtub Virgin Mary beamed serenely from her shell. After the State of California shut down Tony Cornero's gambling ships, Loretta'd been evicted from his bungalow on Olive Street. She'd pilfered but two items to remind her she'd survived. She'd kept a dresser and that statue of the Blessed Virgin Mary. It cast a shadow on the paving bricks traversing the dichondra at Loretta's place on Barton Street.

A lot of people laughed.

Loretta didn't care. The plaster statue soothed her soul, and it reminded her that people could be pure, unlike herself. Some days she'd stop to pay respects and mutter off a Hail Mary, because Loretta knew how evil she could be.

She worked for Martin Aviation now. The sale of Rico's Auburn last July netted enough for a significant down payment.

Her Martin paychecks might be modest, but they covered the expenses on her stick-and-stucco bungalow in central Santa Ana. Loretta glanced down at her wristwatch. Five minutes slow. She set it five minutes ahead, knowing tomorrow she'd reset it once again. It was that watch she'd bought for Javy, its face resembling a compass. It had passed down to her daughter, who had gifted it to Willie. Loretta didn't plan on giving it away, ever again. She needed things that were consistent in her life. She wound the stem. *Gentleman's wristwatches felt so right at the factory*, she thought.

Loretta took a sip of coffee. Set it down next to this week's *Life* Magazine, kicked off her mules and sprawled her legs across the chesterfield. KVOE was on the air, playing swing tunes from New York. Glenn Miller. After that came Dinah Shore's *I'll Walk Alone*.

She tuned it up.

She shut her eyes, and she relaxed, humming along with Dinah Shore. Soft footsteps padded down her hallway, Elenita's. The five-year-old carried her shoebox full of cutout paper dolls Loretta'd snipped out from the pages of September's *Jack and Jill.*

The volume on Loretta's radio went down without her touching it.

A soft palm nudged her forehead.

The girl's voice whispered, "Mama?"

Loretta opened up her eyes.

"Well, hello there, polar bear. "Loretta glanced up at her daughter. This child always seemed so cheerful and precocious. Loretta shook herself awake.

"Mama?" Elenita asked."

"Yes, what is it, sweetie?"

"How come I don't have a daddy?" The little girl folded her arms.

Loretta jolted to attention. She sat straight up on the sofa, and her heart stopped. She blinked. Sooner or later this had to happen.

She stood. She made her way toward Tony's beat-up wooden dresser. She held her breath, and there she pulled the top drawer open once again. She unwrapped the faded tissue on a cheap black-and-white photograph still framed with its rope border on a lacquered teakwood frame from a studio somewhere in Honolulu.

Loretta gave the dusty photo in its frame to Elenita.

A sailor smiled back through the glass, proud, and with huge muscular arms crossing his chest inside a boiler room with massive pipes and valves. The man's big shoulders looked as wide as those B-26 Marauders Loretta wired up at Martin Aviation.

Willie appeared as if he'd finally found a place where he belonged. His eyes were serious and level like he knew his occupation. In one corner on a white circular lifering, Loretta read the awful words, *U. S. S. Arizona*.

She closed her eyes.

"Is this my daddy?"

"The Navy mailed it to me after Willie died."

"Did you love Daddy?"

"I reckon on a few occasions," said Loretta.

Elenita pressed a chubby finger against the glass. Studied his features. "Was Daddy a good man?"

Loretta sighed. "Honey, are any of us good?" She looked away. And then she shrugged. She wound her Elgin wristwatch even tighter. She pulled Elenita close. Loretta hugged her.

Extra hard.

With her free hand, Loretta dialed up her Sears Silvertone radio. Clarinet this time, instead of the old Mexican *marimba*. Artie Shaw was playing *Frenesí*.

Again.

THE END

DRAMATIS PERSONAE

Characters in *italics* are fictitious. Characters in **bold** were real people.

Atlas, Charles (nee Angelo Siciliano) – 1892-1972 – Italian-American bodybuilder and self-proclaimed "World's Most Perfectly Developed Man" made famous through magazine and comic book ads promoting his mail-order body-building courses and techniques.

Autry, Gene (nee Orvon Grove Autry) – 1907-1998 – Texas-born rodeo performer, songwriter, country and western singer and movie star nicknamed The Singing Cowboy who later Owned a television station and the California Angels baseball team.

Brown, Buster – 1902-19xx – Comic book character created in 1902 by Richard Outcault adopted as mascot of Brown Shoe Company in 1904.

Browne, Father Patrick – 18xx-19xx – Dublin-born priest of Saint Boniface Catholic Church in Anaheim during the 1920's and 1930's.

Buffum, Charles Abel – 1870-1936 – Illinois-born businessman and mayor of Long Beach from 1921-1924. In 1904, Charles and his brother Edwin purchased Schilling Brothers Mercantile Store. They built it into a chain of high-end department stores throughout Los Angeles, Orange, and San Diego Counties. His daughter, Dorothy married Los Angeles Times heir Norman Chandler and like her father became a well-known Southern California philanthropist.

Cornero, Tony "Tony the Hat", "The Admiral" – 1899-1955 – Southern California bootlegging and gambling entrepreneur. Partner in the *S. S. Rex* and *S. S. Tango* gambling ships. Later founded the Stardust Casino in Las Vegas

Davis, Bette nee Ruth Elizabeth Davis – 1908-1989 – New England-born Academy Award winning American actress known for playing unsympathetic characters

DeMille, Cecil Blount – 1881-1959 – Pioneer American filmmaker who made 70 features for Paramount Studios between 1914 and 1958. The most commercially successful producer-director in film history, his films were known for their epic scale and lavish spectacle.

Dye, Clark – 1904-1993 – Texas-born owner operator of Santa Ana hardware store. (In reality his store did not open until 1946.)

Fitts, Buron Rogers – 1895-1973 – Texas-born 29th lieutenant governor of California from 1927-1928 and thereafter Los Angeles County District Attorney until 1940. Wounded in 1937 by volley of shots fired through his car windshield in a case that was never solved.

Fonda, Henry Jaynes – 1905-1982 – Nebraska-born Academy Award winning American film actor

Garbo, Greta nee Greta Lovisa Gustafsson –1905-1990 – Swedist-born movie actress known for portrayal of tragic film characters and understated performances.

Kent, Mildred – 1888-19xx –fictitious Santa Ana resident and socialite

Laird, Vivian – 19xx-19xx – Southern California nightclub operator owned Vivian Laird's and The Bohemia in Long Beach, The South Seas on Manchester Boulevard southeast of Anaheim, and the Garden of Allah in Seal Beach.

Louis, Joseph Barrow "Joe Louis the Brown Bomber" – 1914-1981 – Alabama-born American professional boxer and from, 1937-1949 world heavyweight champion considered in his era to be the greatest heavyweight boxer of all time.

Malone, Jack "Suicide Jack" – 1910-1938 – fictitious Singapore-born hustler.

Miller, Alton Glenn – 1904-1944 – Iowa-born big band leader and trombonist who disappeared over the English Channel while traveling to entertain American troops stationed in France.

Norton, Lawrence Richard – 1894-1938 – fictitious orchard owner near Placentia, California

Norton, Priscilla – 1898-1998 – fictitious wife of Richard Norton

O'Reilly, Miguel –– 1890-19xx – fictitious Mexican-born father of Willie O'Toole and grandson of San Patricio warrior.

O'Toole, Guillermo Juan "Willie" – 1919-1942 – fictitious Santa Ana busboy and Navy recruit.

O'Toole, Maria Juana – 1900-1936 – fictitious mother of Willie O'Toole.

O'Toole, Stanley – 1890-19xx – fictitious stepfather of Willie O'Toole.

Quinn, Anthony nee Manuel Antonio Rodolfo Quinn Oaxaca – 1915-2001 – Chihuahua-born American actor active 1936 until his death. Won Oscar for Best Supporting Actor twice, for *Viva Zapata!* in 1952 and *Lust for Life* in 1956.

Santa Anna y Pérez de Lebrón, Antonio de Padua María Severino López de – 1794-1876 – Mexican military General and political leader who commanded Mexican forces fighting against United States in 1848 Mexican-American War.

Sariñana, Josefina – 19xx-19xx – Proprietor of fictitious Josefina's Tamales, (loosely based on Sariñana's Tamale Factory in Santa Ana although Sariñana's, the inspiration for Josefina's was not founded until 1939)

Shaw, Artie nee Arthur Jacob Arshawsky – 1910-2004 – 1930's and 40's big band swing leader, clarinet player, and actor.

Shore, Dinah nee Fanye Rose Shore – 1916-1994 – American singer and actress and the top charting female vocalist of the 1940's.

Smith, Bessie – 1894-1937 – 1920's pioneer black jazz vocalist known as the "Empress of the Blues" and the most popular blues singer of her era

Teagarden, Weldon Leo "Jack" – 1905-1964– Texas-born trombonist, singer, and band leader who often played aside his lifelong friend Louis Armstrong.

Tramontano, Enrico – 1898-1938 – fictitious Southern California playboy and gangster.

Valenzuela, Elena – 1921-1938 – fictitious daughter of Loretta Valenzuela

Valenzuela, Javier (Javy) – 1904-1932 – butcher, meatpacker, and father of Elena Valenzuela

Valenzuela, Loretta, "Tight Sweater Loretta" – 1907-19xx – cigarette girl, aircraft electrician and mother of Elena Valenzuela

Wills, Robert "Bob", – 1905-1975 – Leader and fiddle player of Western swing bands including the Light Crust Doughboys and later Bob Wills and His Texas Playboys

Velasco, José – 1908-1985– fictitious Filipino barber in Santa Ana and friend of Willie's.

AUTHOR Q&A

1. **What in your life prepared you to be a writer? And when did you begin writing fiction?**
   I began writing fiction 25 years ago after receiving a death threat from an insurance company. Having found success as a civil engineer after the Northridge Earthquake locating and documenting earthquake damage and presenting the engineering basis for repair claims, I encountered a rogue adjuster who preferred to take the low road. That taste of corruption was the seed from which *my Red Car Noir series* emerged.

   Eventually, California Insurance Commissioner, Charles Quackenbush, was forced to resign for taking payoffs from insurance companies he'd been elected to police. At last, the corruption in California became evident. But friends, under the spell of what psychologists call "authority bias," were hesitant to admit insurance companies were so dishonest. Figuring novels were a sneaky way to tell the truth to people who seemed angry about having their beliefs called into question, I took up writing fiction. It has taken me decades to become a decent writer, but I made so many writer friends I kept at it for years. Plus, I had to find out what was going to happen to my characters.

2. ***Cigarette Girl* is your second *Red Car Noir* novel. Is this a sequel to your first, *The Anaheim Beauties Valencia Queen*, or do both books stand alone?**
Both books stand alone although the settings overlap. Having grown up in La Cañada Flintridge, just north of Glendale, California, I'm a huge James M. Cain fan. I love his three classics, *Double Indemnity, The Postman Always Rings Twice and Mildred Pierce,* all set in and around Glendale, California and written before Cain waded off into novels about opera. The dilemma with a noir series is your protagonist can't die unless, of course it is the last book of the series. This means the plots are more predictable, and the tension is diminished. In a Raymond Chandler novel (and I love his stuff) you know throughout the book that Philip Marlowe lives. The dame will disappoint him, and you won't be sure until the last page just who did the dirty deed. You are carried by the voice and Philip Marlowe's truthful cynicism. In a stand-alone, there's liberty for unexpected endings. This can make them fun to read and fun to write.

3. **How long did it take to research and write *Cigarette Girl?***
This one took about a year. I'd written *Anaheim Beauties* set in 1924 in Anaheim, and I wanted a companion to be set in Santa Ana. I used the flood to kick it off, because I'd learned that during the 1926 Saint Francis Dam disaster there were hundreds of found corpses that have never

been identified. These were largely migrant workers. I wanted to know more about their stories, and I wanted to give one of them a face.

In the course of research, I became fascinated with the history of gambling in Orange County, both the Charlie Boards and the gambling ships that left from Seal Beach. I hadn't known that Seal Beach was the original "Sin City," before Tony Cornero and Bugsy Siegel picked up their chips and moved to Vegas.

4. **Speaking of research, you ground your reader with accuracy. A good number of people, places, and events are real. Do you do all your research on your own? And as a writer, how does research impact your process?**

   I do most of my own research. Over my lifetime I've acquired a large collection of old maps, pictures, and esoteric data, plus connections that help put forgotten faces and places at my fingertips. A writer never knows what information can launch a story in new directions. I like my research to surprise me. I found a picture of a matchbook from *The Tango,* another from Vivian Laird's Garden of Allah in Seal Beach, and a Charlie Board in rather poor condition. I bought an old map of Orange County from the thirties off of Ebay. I threw them all into the pot and hoped a story might come together. In this case I believe that I got lucky.

   I strive for authenticity, but sometimes have to take some liberties. Clark Dye Hardware and Josefina's (loosely based on Sariñana's) did not exist in 1938. But I try to find the details to make stories come alive, even to the point that I immerse myself in music of the era.

5. **Please give us a sense of what you consider your most important themes and what you hope your readers take away from reading your work.**
   I write a lot about moral injury. It is an underlying theme of much of noir and a reason noir was and is popular with GI's. In the Sixties, college graduates became convinced they were more virtuous than their parents. Prior to Vietnam, the opposite was true. GI's had *killed people* in battle, something their parents and professors had rarely done, and the daughters had some stories to tell, too. Veterans can't afford to virtue signal. They know themselves too well. They've been humbled. And I think humbled people have a lot to teach us. To quote Loretta, "Honey, are any of us good?"

6. **As a writer, do you outline? And do you know the story arc and the ending of the book when you sit down to write, or does it develop as you go?**
   I'm more of an organic seat of the pants writer than an outline writer. The one thing I outline is a thorough historical timeline to keep my facts straight, and the details of my characters. Then I turn them loose and hope my characters surprise me. I had an ending in mind for Willie, but it didn't solidify until I'd written past the midpoint. Then it finally came together. I had a sense it might be dark. *Anaheim Beauties* was more upbeat. This one was dark, but it felt true to the characters I'd written.

7. **Willie, Loretta, Suicide Jack – how real were your main characters to you? What does an author have to feel to be able to breathe life into their characters?**
As an organic writer I try to get into my characters' minds the same way a method actor tries to become their character. This can be challenging when not all of my characters are nice people. As long as I am clear about what each character wants more than life itself, the story flows and writes itself. When I lose track of what each character wants, writers block happens, and I need to spend some more time with my characters.

8. **As the storyteller, you chose to let Willie die. Why?**
I see Willie as a member of the "Greatest Generation." He grew up innocent, became jaded, and reluctantly became tough, but found some sort of redemption in his fate. I also wanted an ending where it clearly didn't matter what his race was. Perhaps it even added to his stature. In the end, he was American in the best sense of the word.

9. **Often writers pit good against evil. You do this, but it does not seem black and white. There is a lot of shading. Do you agree with this assessment? Why?**
I agree with this assessment. I strive for honest writing, which means no character is all good or all evil. My goal is to show reality and allow the reader to ask and answer their own questions. I try very hard to make my readers think without telling them what to think. I hope my novel's gift to readers is to help them see and cope with gray in a world presenting itself as black and white.

10. **Why did you end the novel the way you did?**
I wanted to end with ambiguity. We live in an era where moral certainty is polarizing and destroying our good country from within. I grew up after World War II on a street where there were many men who'd killed people in battle. These men were capable of evil. But they also could forgive. Forgiveness is a skill that most Americans have lost.

11. **What do you see as the most important role of history? Do you think that we have enough of a sense of it in today's society?**
History is how we learn from our mistakes, and to quote George Santayana, those who cannot remember the past are condemned to repeat it. I am concerned we're not remembering our past. Further, when our collective past is sliced and diced into one-thousand different narratives, we have no sense of who we are as individuals and are ripe for exploitation.

    This is why I'm quite concerned about our iconoclastic times. We are almost being ordered to forget where we have come from. The job of history is to teach us, not to flatter those in charge. When our history is stolen we have no compass.

12. **You call your genre "Red Car Noir." Where does this name come from? What can a reader expect from a Red Car Noir novel?**
I wanted a name to brand the novels I've written and am writing. I boiled it down to "Southern California-based historical fiction chronicling the dark side of

the American Dream," which is a mouthful. I needed something catchier and shorter. The Red Car reference is to that period of Southern California history (1901-1961) where the Pacific Electric Red Car trolleys ran throughout Los Angeles. A few works extend into the early 1970's. The Kennedy Assassination, Vietnam, and Watergate represent the period's sunset. But the bulk of my work is set within the early 1900's, an era underrepresented in our literature.

As for "noir," the genre has both a broad definition and a narrow one, with film-noir being narrower than roman noir or neo-noir. My focus on realism, on the dark side of the American dream, with *femmes fatales* and protagonists who aren't detectives but are victimized by a system that is more corrupt than they are, fits within the broad but not the narrow definition. My primary departure from the full-blown film-noir genre is my self-destructive protagonists don't always die or go to prison. Amidst tragedy, some find a sadder-but-wiser resolution with jaded resignation and contentment.

Red Car Noir is more like neo-noir. The movie *Chinatown* comes to mind. Jake Gittes makes it out of Chinatown, but with scars, and there are characters who never make it out.

13. **Are there other Red Car Noir novels in the works?**
A third work, *The Lady with the Shattered Foundation* is in the works set in the aftermath of the 1932 Long Beach Earthquake.

14. I'm also halfway through the second installment of my *Angeltown* trilogy set in the early 1900's, amidst labor wars, the Salton Sea floods, and the Owens Valley Aqueduct. The history of Los Angeles is wrapped up in its water, and being a water engineer, I feel compelled to tell the story. The first installment, *Angeltown,* is ready to go to press and deals with all the dirty tricks that brought Los Angeles their water. The story culminates in the bombing of the Los Angeles Times Building in October 1910 where 22 people were murdered.

    Two further volumes, *Edendale,* and *Hollywoodland* are also in the works, taking the saga of Los Angeles into the early 1930's through the Saint Francis Dam disaster and the demise of William Mulholland. I'm 30,000 words into writing *Edendale,* and enjoying it.

QUESTIONS FOR DISCUSSION

1. Willie is nineteen years old when we meet him. Would you describe him as a man or a boy? Why?

2. What were you like at nineteen? What support systems did you have in place? How independent were you? How equipped to handle life?

3. In what ways was the Orange County of 1938 similar to or different from Orange County today?

4. What role does the Great Depression play in this story?

5. How does the staccato sentence structure impact the novella's tone. Did it seem the author deviated from this structure in places, and if so, why do you think the author might have done so?

6. Why do you think Elena gave Willie her Papi's watch? What do you think the watch meant to Willie? In what ways is the watch a symbol of something greater?

7. Why do the farmers deny they ever had a barn? What do you think of Willie's response? How might you have responded?
8. In one word, describe the farmers' attitude toward the migrants. Discuss what this says about the farmers.
9. The farmer's wife refers to Willie as a half-breed. What does his response tell you?
10. Willie's world is upended when he learns his heritage is not what he was told? What might be your reaction to such a discovery?
11. We've all known people like Mildred. How might you describe her?
12. What makes someone a parent?
13. Despite their physical similarities, there are marked differences between Elena and Loretta. What do these differences immediately tell you?
14. Loretta is immediately willing to help Willie? Why? Why do you think Willie is so accepting of her help?
15. What do you think caused so much hardness in Loretta?
16. What edge does Loretta have over Willie? What edge does he have over her?
17. Sometimes people make each other stronger, and sometimes they diminish each other. Which would you say is the case for Willie and Loretta?
18. What role does the money made from the Charley Boards have in the story?

19. Do you think Charley Boards should be legal or illegal? Why or why not?

20. There are many reasons for people to have sex. Why do Willie and Loretta do so?

21. Loretta works for the people who killed her husband. What do you think it takes to do this?

22. Moral injury in psychology refers to an injury to an individual's moral conscience resulting from an act of perceived moral transgression which produces profound emotional shame. Do you feel any characters experienced moral injury? In what way were they impacted?

23. As Willie comes to viscerally understand the place of Mexicans in Orange County, he initially holds in his anger. What puts him over the edge?

24. What ramifications did Willie face because of his mixed race? Discuss how society treats people of mixed race today.

25. Compare the shadow culture inhabited by Suicide Jack with that inhabited by Elena and *Abuelo*. In what ways might living in the shadows impact one's life?

26. Why would there be such a discrepancy between the newspaper report of how Norton died and how he actually died? How often do you find yourself questioning what is said in the media?

27. Despite all he goes through, Willie craves respect and believes in honor. What do these two words mean to you? What role do they play in your life?

28. At what point did you suspect Loretta might be pregnant?

29. What does it say about Willie that he is unable to kill? Why do you think it is easier for Loretta?

30. Can you imagaine any circumstances in which you could be as seemingly callous as Loretta? And is she really callous?

31. Why do you think Willie turns to Stan? When Stan comes through for him, how might that have impacted Willie? Discuss a time when someone came through for you unexpectedly – or let you down.

32. Between 1929 and 1936, 400,000 to 2,000,000 Mexicans and Mexican Americans were deported from the southwestern United States, often with raids and paramilitary operations cooridinated between federal and local law enforcement. By the end of the "Mexican Repatriation", known in Mexico as *La Repatriacion*, roughly a third of all Hispanics in the United States had been deported into Mexico. An estimated 60% of those deported were birthright U.S. citizens. José David Orozco described on his L.A. radio station "women crying in the streets when not finding their husbands" after deportation sweeps. To what extent were you aware of the extent of *La Repatriacion*?

33. Discuss the ways you feel it *La Repatriacion* impacted Willie and other characters in the story.

34. What do you think the will to survive did to Loretta's soul?

35. At the conclusion of the novel, it seems Loretta has stopped smoking. Did you notice? Why do you think she quit?

36. Were you suspecting the ending? How did you feel about it?

37. How would you answer Loretta's question to Elenita, "Honey are any of us good?"

38. In your opinion was Willie a good man?

39. In your opinion was Loretta a good woman?

ACKNOWLEDGMENTS

If I thanked everyone who in some manner contributed to this book, the names would not fill a dozen pages. I am truly very fortunate. But there are six individuals I wish to thank profusely for their patience, wisdom, guidance, and contributions to this book.

1. To Dennis Coplan, author, who helped me crystalize the story.
2. To Louella Nelson, author, teacher, and writing mentor, who has been mentoring my writing since the Clinton Administration.
3. To Janet Simcic, author and critique group leader, who kept nagging me to publish this one too.
4. To Maddie Margarita, author, and the foremost cheerleader for authors in Orange County, California, who convinced me that my writing didn't suck.
5. To Gwyn Snider who masterminded the artwork and the cover.

6. To Antoinette Kuritz, publicist and La Jolla Writers Conference founder, who helped to get the word out on this book.

ABOUT THE AUTHOR

D. J. Phinney is an Air Force veteran and a licensed civil and mechanical engineer who has been responsible for design and construction of more than $100 million in water and wastewater infrastructure in California and Arizona.

A Southern California native with a passion for history and construction, Mr. Phinney turned to writing fiction, following the Northridge Earthquake, when a death threat from an insurance company helped him see fiction as a sneaky way to write about the truth. *The Cigarette Girl on the Tango* is his second Red Car Noir novel and a companion to *The Anaheim Beauties Valencia Queen* also set in old Orange County. When not writing, Mr. Phinney spends time with his wife of 40 years, their grown son, their grandchildren and their golden retriever. Or he can be found exploring local history in anticipation of completing his next Red Car Noir adventure.

CPSIA information can be obtained
at www.ICGtesting.com
Printed in the USA
LVHW021002210321
682022LV00008B/1657

9 781732 903418